KU-104-875

2018

Thought you might like
to check out your literary
competition!
Love,
Anne-Marie
xxx

Kristen Nairn

A SORRY AFFAIR

AUSTIN MACAULEY
PUBLISHERS LTD.

Copyright © Kristen Nairn (2017)

The right of Kristen Nairn to be identified as author of this work has been asserted by him in accordance with section 77 and 78 of the Copyright, Designs and Patents Act 1988.

All rights reserved. No part of this publication may be reproduced, stored in a retrieval system, or transmitted in any form or by any means, electronic, mechanical, photocopying, recording, or otherwise, without the prior permission of the publishers.

Any person who commits any unauthorized act in relation to this publication may be liable to criminal prosecution and civil claims for damages.

A CIP catalogue record for this title is available from the British Library.
ISBN 9781787104006 (Paperback)
ISBN 9781787104013 (E-Book)
www.austinmacauley.com

First Published (2017)
Austin Macauley Publishers Ltd.
25 Canada Square
Canary Wharf
London
E14 5LQ

Chapter 1
Abbi

She stood outside the door, her heart pounding so hard in her chest, she thought she would wake the neighbours and shatter the peace and quiet which was already closing in on her. She glanced sideways at the window, looking for some clue about the lives of the occupants inside. It was a typical Victorian terraced building in a typical quiet, leafy suburban street. She could picture it inside. Bay windows, high ceilings, sanded floors, probably painted in whites and neutrals. The occupants were most likely drinking coffee and reading the Sunday papers in their spacious, airy kitchen; content and secure in their mutual silence, unaware that things were about to change forever for them. One ring of the doorbell, and their peaceful, calm Sunday morning routine would be shattered.

She hesitated, finger hovering over the doorbell. What would an outsider think? Did she look odd, shifty? She panicked. Had she really thought this through? She jumped at the sound of the doorbell. She looked at her finger pressing hard on it. It seemed strangely disconnected to her body. Had she really meant to push the doorbell? Too late now. She could hear muffled voices and soft footsteps on the wooden floors. Someone rummaging for keys on the other side. A female voice, laughing, shouting through the door, 'Sorry, won't be a moment.'

A movement to her right caught her eye. She turned her head slowly, and saw him. A stunned, horrified look on his face. Then suddenly, he sprang into action, racing through to the hall, shouting, 'No! Jen, no! Leave it. I'll get it, it's for me.'

Too late.Jen had opened the door. She was beautiful! Mack hadn't mentioned how beautiful she was. She hadn't expected it. Jen looked tiny, framed in the doorway, shielding her eyes from the morning sun. She was still in her nightclothes by the look of it. Her blond hair tumbling messily to her shoulders. Had they just had sex? She smiled, revealing a row of perfect white teeth. A polite, but confused smile, which soon froze as he appeared behind her, almost pushing her back out of the way.

'What is it, what's going?' she asked, frowning.

'Jen, go back in, let me deal with this, I know what this is about.'

***

One month later, they sat across from each other, two mugs of coffee, untouched between them. Her whole body felt heavy and sluggish, immobilising her. The silence between them was stifling. She felt she couldn't be the first to speak. She was the guilty party and had been summoned here. She wasn't allowed to have any control over how this meeting would go. She waited. And waited, until finally the silence was broken.

A clear, strong voice cut through the hissing of the coffee machine in the background.

'You stole everything; my life, my plans, my dreams, my hopes. My fiancée. He was *my* fiancée. We were going to be married. But you knew that didn't you? You knew from the first moment you met him a year ago that he wasn't yours to take. I'm not here to ask why, or hear your side of the story. I'm not interested. I'm not here to forgive you. I just had to see what kind of person would do that to another.'

Abbi stared at the coffee in front of her. Hot tears stung her eyes. A lump formed at the back of her throat, preventing her from talking. Strictly speaking, it wasn't true. She had actually met him four years ago, and yes, she had known then that he had a girlfriend, but she had no idea he still had a girlfriend, *a fiancée*, when she met him again this time round, although admittedly, she hadn't asked. Now wasn't the time to argue the point though. She thought back to the moment she had first met him.

***

It was late, dark and cold as she stood at the bus stop; checking her watch every few moments, willing the bus to come early. The climate in Edinburgh never seemed to change. The long streets made perfect wind tunnels, and the temperature was permanently subzero from August until April. Tonight was no exception. The ice cold wind bit into her cheeks and made her eyes water. It was that strange time of night, when the mainstream pubs were closing and you fell into one of two camps. Those that headed home, to a cup of tea and a warm bed, and those that headed for the clubs. Tonight, she was in the first camp. It was too cold and she didn't relish the prospect of falling out of some night club, sweat turning to ice, chilling her to the bone, as she faced the long walk home in the absence of any available taxis.

She pulled her coat tighter around her, stamping her feet to keep out the cold. A group of rowdy men were heading down the hill, jostling each other. She caught snippets of their conversation as they came closer.

'Awe, come on man, you're such a woose. What's happened to you? This is supposed tae be a night out wi' the boys and yur headed back tae the wee woman already. Come on man, yur no even married yet. She'll be fast asleep anyway, she'll no even notice whit time yi get hame.'

'Aye, either that she'll be shagging that neighbour of yours, so either way she'll no be fussed about you coming home.'

The group laughed.

'Fuck off. Just because women give you the perpetual body swerve any time you go near them. Right! Here I am. This is my bus stop. You guys go on, I'll see you on Wednesday at training.'

'Assuming the missus lets you out to play for an hour. Will ye be allowed to come for a pint afterwards?'

'Fuck off! You'll not be as cocky when your flat on your arse after a hard tackle or two.'

He sighed to himself and pulled the collar of his coat up as the others carried on their way. He looked over at her and smiled apologetically. A gorgeous smile. 'Sorry about that. I only swear when I'm out with them. They're a bad influence.'

'That's ok. I'm used to it. My course is mainly guys. I'm not sure they're capable of constructing a sentence without at least one swear word.'

He nodded, indicating he understood. What're you studying?'

'Physics.'

'Whoah. Some course. Where's that?'

'Edinburgh Uni.'

He nodded again, 'Nice. What'll you do with a degree in physics then?' He came and sat nearer her.

'Hmm, not sure. I'm thinking of doing a PhD so that'll buy me some time before I need to think about getting a real job.'

'Good plan. Think an honours year is enough for me. I'm Mack by the way,' he said, holding out his hand.

'And your first name?' She asked, shaking his hand.

'Mack! Short for MacKenzie.' He gave get a lopsided grin. 'Bit wanky I know.'

'Hi MacKenzie. I'm Abbi. And it's Ok. The name I mean. MacKenzie's good,' her heart skipped a beat as he continued to smile at her.

'Mmm, I think my mum and dad did it to spite me.'

She raised her eyebrows inquisitively, 'how so?'

'Well,' he leaned closer and said in hushed tones, 'I'm a third child. First is called John, second is Claire, both pretty safe. Boring even. Then me, MacKenzie. I'm pretty sure I wasn't planned and they were both so pissed off at having a third child that they decided to make my life as miserable as theirs, and give me a naff name.'

'Right.' She couldn't really think of anything to say. They sat in silence for a moment or two. She checked her watch and reckoned the bus would be another five minutes at least.

'Of course, it could be the complete opposite. It could be that they regretted giving your brother and sister boring names and decided to be more adventurous with you,' she said.

'Yeah, maybe. I never thought of it like that.'

'So what's your honors going to be in then?'

'Maths. Dull as fuck.'

'At Edinburgh uni?'

'Yep.'

'Oh, right, I'm surprised we haven't crossed paths. We shared modules with some of the maths lot in the beginning.'

'Yeah,' he grinned, leaning in close again, slightly unsteady from too much alcohol, 'You're assuming I went to lectures.'

She could feel the heat of his breath on her cheeks and caught the faint smell of his aftershave. 'Cigarette?' he said, pulling out a packet and offering her one.

She shook her head, 'No thanks.'

'Don't smoke? No, I shouldn't either,' he said, putting the packet back in his pocket. 'I only have the odd one, but I always feel shit in the morning. Oh, here we go,' he said nodding to the bus as it rounded the corner. 'This is me.'

'And me.'

He followed her as she found a seat and sat next to her, just naturally assuming she had no objection, with the cockiness that came with such good looks, no doubt.

'Where are you headed?'

'Marchmont. And you?'

'Bit further up. Causewayside.'

They parted just as suddenly as they had met. She got up at her stop and said, 'bye then Mack.'

'Yeah, bye then,' he smiled, getting up to let her out of her seat. 'Nice meeting you Abbi. Might see you around the physics department.'

'Yeah, maybe.'

She gave him as much time and opportunity as she could to ask for her number, but he just raised his eyebrows and smirked. She moved swiftly to get off the bus, feeling slightly humiliated. Had he known she hoped he'd ask for her number? She had thought there had been a spark between them, some sort of attraction. She didn't often feel it, but she had on this occasion. She thought back to the conversation she'd heard earlier, something about him not being married yet. She had thought it was just banter, but maybe he had a girlfriend. Maybe he flirted with everyone, again, a natural right of passage for the good looking.

She was pretty sure he was looking out the window at her as the bus drew away, but she turned her back on him, pulled her hat over her head, and marched purposefully off in the other direction. *Cocky bastard* she thought to herself. She may not be very experienced in love, but one thing she was certain of, she would never let a guy walk all over her. She knew enough about cocky pricks and what they were capable of. God knows she was surrounded by them every day. Either that or physics nerds who wouldn't notice her if she walked around the lab in her bra and knickers, not unless she was attached to a Van der Graff generator and could offer a rational alternative theory to explain the meaning of black holes.

She had to admit, she fully expected see him loitering about the physics department, pretending to bump into her *by accident*, quoting some pathetic excuse about waiting for a mate. But no.

A few days turned into a few weeks, then months. She pushed her disappointment deep down inside her, scolding herself for being so stupid. *Why would anyone like him be interested in her?* Eventually she stopped looking for him

11

and after a year, reasoned he must have completed his honors year by now and had probably moved to London to take up some job in the City.

Cast her mind forward three years. One disastrous relationship under her belt and drowning her sorrows at some dull student party. A voice behind her made her jump.

'So how's the PhD going?'

She knew, without turning round, he was smirking. She turned as slowly as she could, convinced he would see her heart beating beneath her shirt. She tried to remain calm, to maintain her poise. She smiled and paused a moment, as if trying to recall him. She knew fine who he was, and he knew she knew. As predicted, he had a smirk on his face, which turned into a grin.

'Mack! An ice cold night and a short bus journey a few years ago,' he reminded her.

She nodded, 'I know, I remember now,' she smiled, 'and it's almost finished. I'm writing my thesis now. So what did you do with the math. s?'

'Teacher!'

'No way! Really?'

He looked a bit sheepish. 'Yeah, not very glamorous I know. I'm not sure I'll stick at it forever, but it'll do for now. What about you, what are you going to do next?'

'I'm not sure. Take one big holiday that's for sure, then there's a few places I'd like to work, assuming there's jobs.'

He nodded, finished his beer and said, 'Look, I don't know about you but I'm thinking this party isn't going to get any better. The only thing marginally worse would be if we were in fancy dress. I'm guessing any minute now someone's going to suggest charades or a drinking game, just to totally kill the idea that there's any fun to be had

12

here. What do you say we go off in search of something a bit more lively, assuming of course this isn't your party and I haven't deeply offended you.'

She laughed, despite her reservations. He had a mischievous glint in his eyes and a playfulness which was contagious.

'No, it's not my party and yes it is as dull as dishwater. Where do you have in mind?'

'Well,' he said leaning close to her, in exactly the same way he'd done all those years ago 'a visit to Grey friar's graveyard would be more fun than this,' and placing a hand on the small of her back, ushered her to the door, collecting their coats on the way.

She honestly didn't think to ask in the days and months that followed if he had a girlfriend. Why would she? Surely, in most cases when two people meet, get on well and start dating, the assumption is that both are single? She had asked herself this many times, perhaps trying to absolve herself of guilt and responsibility. She wanted to ask this question now, of the beautiful Jen, sitting across from her, staring at her.

Admittedly, she wasn't the most practiced when it came to relationships, but surely even the most experienced person wouldn't have seen this coming.

She wanted to tell Jen that *her* life, *her* hopes and *her* dreams had been shattered too, but this meeting wasn't about her. There was no point. Why should Jen care?

Even now, she couldn't find it in her heart to hate him. Maybe one day she would. Once she stopped loving him, but she wasn't ready for that yet. Clearly Jen hadn't stopped loving him either. That's why she was so angry and hurt at this moment.

He was very easy to love. He was funny, good looking and had a great body, but it was more than that. He was charming, without being sleazy, and there was something exciting about him. He was one of those people that others were naturally drawn to. Everyone wanted to be near him and to be part of his group. You could almost feel the energy in a room lift when he walked in. He was just one of those people who naturally assumed the control and command position in a group, and tended to remain there all evening, without really having to work too hard at it. People were drawn to him like the proverbial moths to a flame.

All of that, combined with his natural sex appeal, made him irresistible. Even now, she could clearly remember the shock waves which rippled through her body when he touched her arm as he chatted to her in the pub that first night.

She remembered leaving the party with him, the pair of them sneaking out, giggling like naughty school kids concealing some private joke.

She looked up at him when they reached the street outside. 'Grey friar's it is then? I hope you're not easily scared,' she teased.

'Nah, although maybe we should go to Grey friar's pub instead. Bit warmer. What do you say?'

'Ok, sounds good.'

She was surprised a few hours later when the bell rang for last orders. Where had the time gone? She checked her watch and saw him smirk as she did so. Perhaps he was used to having this effect on women.

They finished their drinks and stood up to put their coats on. The wind howled outside and she shivered in anticipation of the cold air which was about to hit her.

She tensed as he reached forward, wrapping his scarf around her neck. 'Suits you,' he said smiling. 'It's my favourite one, but I might let you keep it.'

She tried to take a deep breath to steady herself, but it had the opposite effect as she breathed in his scent and she shuddered, her insides melting just a little, as he tied the scarf in a knot around her neck.

She was touched by this small, simple gesture. She wasn't sure why it meant so much to her, but it did. It was a sign he cared about her on some level. He was looking after her and obviously liked her.

He took her by the elbow, 'Come on let's go before the bear behind the bar decides to kick our asses from here straight into the graveyard.

Her heart fluttered. They automatically put their heads down to avoid the cold air as they stepped out of the warmth of the pub. He put his arm around her shoulders and pulled her closer to him. She let her body lean into his as they crossed the road.

He laughed as he realised he didn't know where they were going. 'Do you still live in Marchmont?'

'Yes, but not the same flat. You've got a good memory. Do you still live in Causewayside?'

'No, moved up in the world. Stockbridge now.'

'Ooh, very posh,' she teased.

'Yeah, it's ok,' he shrugged, quickly changing the subject. 'I'll see you home. I'd normally suggest we go on somewhere but I have early start tomorrow. In fact, I'm driving and was supposed to be off the drink, shit!'

'Who made those rules?'

'Team rules,' he answered quickly. 'Football. We take it in turns to drive and whoever drives shouldn't drink, although we're all supposed to be taking it easy. We're not getting any younger and the matches are getting harder.'

'Sounds serious. Where are you playing tomorrow?'

'Glasgow. Tough at the best of times.'

She felt a stab of disappointment. A small part of her had hoped he'd invite her back to hers, but for the main, she was relieved. The thought of being with him terrified her. She got the feeling he was pretty experienced and she felt suddenly embarrassed by her lack of experience. *Would it show?* she wondered.

'That's ok,' she said brightly. 'I have the joy of writing a thesis ahead of me all day tomorrow, so I don't think I could cope with any more excitement tonight.'

He tightened his hold on her shoulder and smiled. 'I've never had competition from a physics thesis before.'

She doubted he'd ever had any competition from anything before. She smiled back, 'I'm sure it won't do you any harm to have a bit of healthy competition now and then.'

Before she knew what was happening, he whipped her round to face him and was kissing her. He wrapped one hand around her waist and one round the back of her neck, pulling her head in towards his own, his tongue searching for hers. She responded straight away, forgetting any fears about her lack of experience. He pushed her back gently against a shop door, pressing his body into hers.

She felt a rush of pleasure wash over her body and down her thighs, making her legs go weak. He stopped as suddenly as he had started and rested his forehead on hers.

'I've wanted to do that for three years,' he whispered.

She laughed loudly, 'and here's me thinking you're not cheesy.'

'What?' he grinned, 'It's true! I'll just need to make up for it now,' he said quietly, bringing his lips down on hers again.

She felt as if her body was on fire, despite the bitter wind whipping round them.

He walked her home as promised and they kissed again outside her flat. It took every bit of willpower she had to resist inviting him in for coffee. Eventually, he pulled away and smiled at her, 'Ok, I really must go, otherwise my legendary striking foot will get frostbite.'

She nodded, 'and the most I'll be able to write is a shopping list.'

They kissed again, reluctant to part. 'Keep my scarf. I'll get it back during the week.' He raised his eyebrows, pulled up the collar of his wool jacket and was off. She watched him for a moment or two before reluctantly heading up to her flat.

***

And there it was. She was hooked. None of it her fault. She didn't go seeking him out, chasing him around against his will, asking him in for coffee. She felt powerless to resist, as pathetic as that sounded now. At the time it was utterly romantic. She felt it was fate. It was obviously meant to be, two chance meetings, and now what would follow would be an intensely passionate romance, marriage, children, two cats, a dog and a cottage by the sea.

What would you have done? she wanted to ask this beautiful, heartbroken girl who sat across from her now. *Would you really have asked questions? Would you have instantly mistrusted him enough to ask anything at this stage?*

But there was no point asking this question, because what would inevitably follow would be the obvious question, *Well when did you know?* And *What did you do when you found out? Did you end it instantly?*

She couldn't give the answer that Jen wanted. She couldn't say *Yes, of course, it was over the moment I found out.*

But there's a reason for that. A perfectly sound, understandable reason. *HE LIED! HE FUCKING LIED!* she wanted to yell at Jen and everyone else who had consequently judged her in shocked disapproval.

Why had nobody considered that? Why had no one asked what actually happened? People were quick to judge her and weren't interested in finding out the truth. All they could ask was *How could you be so stupid? Did you honestly not suspect a single thing? How could you possibly not know? Didn't you think it was strange that he'd never asked you back to his flat/meet his parents/ meet his friends?* The list was endless.

No! she wanted to scream. *No, I didn't think it was that odd.* He always said he preferred my flat to his. We got the place to ourselves more often. He didn't stay over at mine more than once or twice a week because he was busy preparing his lessons or training or playing football and besides, I was hectic trying to finish my thesis, and didn't want him to put me off. And the parents/ friends thing? I didn't really give it much thought. I was happy to have him to myself.

And as for the well-meaning friends who came out of the woodwork to say, 'I always knew there was something about him.', 'Too good to be true,' *well fuck you! No good telling me now is there?*

Nobody accused you of being stupid though, did they Jen? Nobody asked you how come you didn't suspect a thing? How could you be engaged to someone and not have an inkling they were up to something? What did you think when he didn't come home two nights a week?

She wanted to ask her these questions, but she knew it would be wrong. She desperately wanted people, but especially Jen, to know the truth, to understand her and possibly forgive her, but the truth would hurt. It would crucify her if she loved him as much as she, Abbi did, and despite what people thought of her, she couldn't do that to another person. She wasn't a horrible, ruthless, home wrecker. She had been innocent in all of this. She had lost the person she loved. She hurt as much as Jen, maybe even more. She had lost friends and had been outcast by family members because of what she'd done. As far as she knew, that hadn't happened to Jen.

She could hear her father's voice ringing in her ears.

'How could you be so stupid? You've got a PhD in physics for God's sake and yet you couldn't see through the oldest lie in the book!' he'd said in disgust when she'd crawled home looking for sympathy, for somewhere she could curl up into a tight ball and shut out the world, where she could be nurtured and healed and brought back to life, like a wounded bird. Unfortunately, everyone else saw a preying mantis, with only one thing in mind.

She'd let everyone down. Her parents had been so proud of her studying physics at University. No one in her family had achieved even a place at University, never mind a degree in physics. But now all that was brushed aside and replaced by the shame she'd brought on her family.

She quickly returned to Edinburgh to escape the oppressive, accusative atmosphere at home. She could hide in her flat, safe in the knowledge that no one would disturb her, until yesterday, until somehow Jen had found her.

The sound of the doorbell had made her jump like a roe deer at the snap of a twig in the forest. She wasn't expecting anyone. It was late afternoon, so even if anyone was calling on her they wouldn't do it now. They'd be at work.

She crept to her bedroom door, opening it slightly to listen for any clues. The bell rang again, causing her heart to hammer against her chest. She stood, rigid, afraid to move in case the floorboards creaked. The only person it could possibly was Mack she thought in panic. She heard a shuffling, keys rattling, then jumped as she saw a piece of paper being pushed through the letter box. She heard heels on the concrete staircase, the sound becoming fainter until she finally heard the heavy front door creak open and slam shut.

She crept over and removed the paper as quietly as possible, worried in case the visitor was somehow still standing there behind the door.

She saw her name on the paper, in neat writing. *Abbi*. Her hands were shaking as she opened it out.

Meet me tomorrow at 1pm, Cafe Rouge. I believe you know where it is! I think you owe me that. Jen.

She ran to the window, scanning the street below for a glimpse of her, but she was nowhere in sight. Her heart was still pounding. She felt sick. What could she say that would make sense of any of this? Of course, she didn't have to go, she didn't really owe her anything. Surely it was Mack who owed her something, owed them both something.

What she really needed was someone to talk to, to ask for advice. Someone on her side. She realised with a sinking feeling, she actually had no one. Mack had been

20

that person recently. She'd seen less of her friends as her relationship with him had intensified. Julia had been her one friend, her confidante in all of this, but Julia had distanced herself once it became apparent that Abbi was continuing the relationship, despite knowing the truth.

***

And now here she was, sitting opposite Jen, the woman whose life she'd wrecked; the woman whose fiancée she'd shared for the past year. She tried her hardest not to think about them both together, sharing a bed together, doing all the things she and Mack had done, sharing the things they'd shared. It was impossible to block out these thoughts though. She knew she was torturing herself, but she was powerless to doing anything about them. A part of her felt she deserved this pain. Jen's beauty did nothing to help her. She wondered if they'd both been in on it, laughing at her behind her back, but she dismissed this thought with a degree of confidence when she saw Jen's red rimmed eyes staring back at her across the table.

What she had once thought of simply as fate working in her favour, she now realised was more a cruel twist of fate. She hadn't planned on going to the party that night. She was supposed to be going to the cinema with two friends, however one pulled out and they agreed to go another night. Her flat mate persuaded them both to come along with him to the party. She went reluctantly, intent on staying for an hour or so, purely to be sociable and pass the time. It was, she reasoned, better than staying in on a Saturday night. And from there, her fate was sealed.

She could remember to the day, the moment she realised she loved him. It was early on in their relationship, but she kept it close to her chest. She felt a mixture of excitement and fear; fear that he didn't feel the same and fear that she'd lose him, although not in the way she eventually had lost him.

In the end, he had said it first. And yes, it had been after they had made love one morning. Perhaps this doesn't count, but for her it had been the words she had been longing to hear. She had no reason to doubt them or his integrity. He had jumped out of bed and headed for the shower before she had a chance to reply, and say the same. He was in a hurry as usual, racing off to get ready for some football game or other. She joined him in the shower, putting her hands around his waist, reaching up to kiss him.

'I love you too,' she smiled, stroking the inside of his thighs, until he couldn't resist any longer.

'Hey, I should say that more often if that's the response I get,' he said smiling down at her.

She started imagining their life together. Married? Possibly. They hadn't discussed this or family before, and up until now, she'd never really thought about it. She'd never really had any particular desire to get married, but now, she could see a different life ahead of her; one which she would share with someone else. She could allow herself to dream of all the things they would do together. She pictured a traditional cosy, domestic scene, where they came home to each other at the end of each day, kissed each other, laughed together, shared stories of their day and went to bed happy each night.

She ran her hands over his body and kissed his chest.

'Oh God, don't,' he groaned, scrunching her hair between his fingers. 'I don't have that much will power. I thought you knew that.'

'I do know that,' she grinned up at him.

22

'You know I'll get hell if I'm late don't you?' he said, nuzzling her neck.

'Mhmm,' she continued, moving her head down his body, covering him in kisses. She felt him tense. She smiled to herself, knowing she had managed to delay him.

This sent shivers down her spine thinking about it even now. She looked up, filled with guilt at having such thoughts, worried that Jen knew exactly what she was thinking about.

On closer inspection, she didn't think so. Jen seemed to have a glazed expression on her face, probably remembering similar events. That thought made her blood run cold. She still couldn't bear to think about Mack and Jen together. It should be Mack sitting here, facing both of them.

Suddenly, Jen refocused, taking Abbi by surprise. Those cold blue eyes were staring at her. She gave Abbi an unnerving smile and leaned forward, pushing the cups of cold, brown liquid to one side. She placed her hands on the table and Abbi could see the indent on her left finger, where a ring had once been.

'So, do you talk? Or do you just sit there like a rabbit in the headlights. Is that what Mack found so appealing? Your wide eyed innocence? His ability to mold you, wrap you round his little finger, have you worship his every move to the extent that you didn't even think to question him? Are you really that gullible?'

'No! And it wasn't like that.' Her throat was dry and sounded hoarse as she tried to speak. She was almost inaudible

Jen looked surprised, 'What was it like then? I'm all ears. That's why I asked you here after all.'

She could feel a lump forming at the back of her throat and hot tears springing to her eyes again. She was powerless to stop it happening.

'Oh please, spare me the tears. I've got enough of my own, I really don't need to see yours as well.'

The tears rolled down her cheeks now. There was no stopping them. A couple at the next table glanced over awkwardly. She wasn't bothered about what anyone else thought. That was the least of her problems.

'I don't think there's anything I can say that will make this any better for you. I can't imagine you're going to believe anything I say. Why would you? I didn't do this deliberately. I didn't set out to hurt you. I didn't even know about you.' She'd found her voice at last and began to talk swiftly, more confidently. She wiped away her tears.

'There's nothing I can say to help you understand what happened because I don't understand it myself. I'm still totally confused and hurt to think the person I fell in love with could do that to me, let alone two of us.'

Jen's face fell. Abbi stopped talking and stared at her. She didn't know! Jen had no idea that she, Abbi, was also in love with him.

'Oh my God,' Abbi whispered. 'It didn't occur to you that I was in love with him, did it? No matter what you think or what he told you, it wasn't some seedy affair. I loved him. He said he loved me.'

She knew by the look on Jen's face, this had come as a complete shock, and that this might be hard for her to hear, but she had a strong desire to tell her the truth, no matter how painful.

'I know you probably won't believe this, but I've never done anything like it before in my life and will never do it again. I'm not some man-eating homewrecker. I haven't

24

even had many boyfriends before, although I know that's no excuse. I know you probably don't want to hear this, but I still love him, despite all he's done. I still can't believe he's done it. Can you tell me honestly, would you have believed the man you were going to marry was capable of cheating on you?'

Jen sighed and slumped back in her chair. Abbi noticed for the first time that this wasn't quite the same woman who had answered the door to her a month ago. On closer inspection, she looked pale and tired. Abbi noticed fine lines around her eyes, which she was sure weren't there normally. Her hair, scraped back from her face, hung limp in a high pony tail.

'No, I guess not.'

'People have asked me how I didn't suspect anything. Why I didn't question things, but I had no reason *not* to believe him. Did it not seem off to you that he stayed out two nights a week?'

Jen flinched, but gave her a cold stare. 'He had always done that. He'd always gone out on a Friday with his friends and usually stayed at one of theirs, and he usually stayed at his friends after training on a Tuesday, so no, I didn't suspect anything, because nothing had changed.'

'Great! So he fitted me in around his normal routine.'

Jen smiled, but there was nothing joyous about it. 'I can ask you the same question. Surely you must have wondered what he did the rest of the week. Surely there must have been times you wanted to see him on a different night? What you're telling me just doesn't add up.'

She sighed, 'It's easy to look back and wonder how come the alarm bells weren't ringing loud and clear, but as I say, I had no reason to be suspicious. You say that it was normal for him to stay out two nights a week. When you first got together didn't you question it? What if you'd found out that he'd actually had another girlfriend and you had unwittingly become the other woman?'

'I would have known,' she spat. 'Are you really saying you played no part in this whole mess?'

'Not to begin with, no.'

'So you do admit that you're not totally innocent?'

Abbi knew she should have just agreed with her and walked away at this point, but she couldn't lie. She still felt she was being treated and judged unfairly.

'When did you find out?' Jen asked.

'About six months ago.'

'And you didn't think to finish it then? I would have thrown him out straight away. No question about it and that's what makes us different. I know you think we're the same and we've both been hard done by, but I didn't have an affair with a man engaged to be married. You could have ended it when you found out and walked away with your head held high.'

Abbi looked away. She was desperate for a coffee now and looked around for the waitress. 'Do you want another coffee?'

'No, I don't want to prolong this anymore than I have to. I just want you to answer the question. Why didn't you end it when you found out?'

Abbi considered her for a moment, not sure whether she should tell her the truth. She wasn't sure if she could handle it. Did she need any further hurt than she'd already suffered? She ordered her coffee. Her need to be understood and have her actions vilified were greater than her need to protect Jen, as harsh as that may sound.

'I saw him more than twice a week, he just didn't stay over.'

She studied Jen closely. She watched as she processed that snippet of information, as it slowly dawned on her that her fiancée had returned to her after spending an evening with his other lover. Her pain was clear to see. Abbi felt guilt gnaw away at her. She couldn't do this. She wanted to put an end to this immediately. She took a sip of her coffee and placing it carefully back in the saucer, started putting her coat on. She'd decided she'd had enough. This wasn't doing either of them any good, and she didn't need to do this. Mack was the only one who could answer Jen's questions.

'Where are you going?' Jen asked, looking alarmed. 'You can't go yet! We haven't finished….please,' she whispered. Suddenly, Jen looked desperate and less in control than she had been earlier. Abbi felt the tables turn. She was the one in control now. Jen needed her. She sighed and removed her coat.

'Okay, I'll try and answer what I can, but are you sure you want to know. I can't help thinking it's only going to hurt you more and that's the last thing I want to do.' She realised how ironic that sounded. Jen hadn't missed the irony either and a look of anger flashed across her face.

'I don't think I can possibly be any more hurt. I need to know the truth. What's the alternative? That I just accept it happened and walk away? Just write it off? I can't do that. I had too much at stake just to do that. I've invested way too much. I've always hated people who talk about needing closure but I understand what they mean now, and I think that's what I need.'

'I don't know much about relationships but I would have thought it was too early for closure. I can't imagine wanting closure just now. It's all still too raw.'

27

Jen gave her that cold, hard stare again, as if she really hated her. Was she struggling to come to terms with the fact that they were talking about the same man.

'I need to know, no matter how much it hurts.'

'OK.' Abbi took a deep breath.

Chapter 2
Jen

The sun was peeking through a gap in the curtain, waking them both up. Mack threw back the covers, rousing her. 'Come on sleepy head, it looks like a great day for a walk.' He was about to jump out of bed but she pulled him back. 'Hey, not so fast. How about just lounging in bed for a while?'

'Beds are for two things and two things only,' he smiled raising an eyebrow.

He looked particularly sexy this morning. His dark, thick hair was tousled and he had a shadow covering his chin, which she loved. They'd made love last night, which had left her feeling aroused this morning and wanting more.

'Well, you're the maths expert, but so far we've only done one of those things today,' she said, pulling him down on top of her and running her hands through his hair as she pulled his head down towards hers. She knew he could always be persuaded to stay in a bed a little longer for the right reason. He rubbed his stubbly chin gently over her shoulders and kissed her neck, making her laugh and squeal at the roughness. She pushed his head further down her body, towards the spot where she knew she would get pleasure. She moaned loudly as his head reached the top of her thighs.

One of the many benefits of having their own place was that they could make as much noise as they liked. Having spent four years of their courtship in student flats, they rarely had much time on their own, which made it difficult to truly explore each other and get a feeling for how far they could go. These past few years had seen an upsurge in their sex life. In fact, moving into their own home had almost renewed and reinvigorated it.

Some things didn't change though. The moment their lovemaking was over, Mack was up and heading for the kitchen to make coffee. He pulled on his pyjama bottoms and a t-shirt from last night and ran his hands through his hair. He grinned at her.

She groaned and rolled over.

'What?' he paused, 'Oh sorry, I've done it again, haven't I?' he said, coming over to her side of the bed. He bent down and kissed her, running his hands up her back.

She was trying to train him, as you would do a puppy, to lie with her for at least five minutes after they'd finished making love.

'Ha, it wasn't that. You just look very sexy when you run your hands through your hair. If you had still been in bed I would have pounced on you again. Now, go and get that coffee before I insist on more sex.'

'I'm one lucky man.' He bounded off towards the kitchen. She lay back and listened to him clattering about, making coffee, getting the cups out. The smell of freshly made coffee filtered through to their bedroom and she reluctantly pulled herself out of bed to go and join him.

Various magazines and work papers were strewn across the kitchen table. He was making scrambled eggs with

toasted bagels and fresh coffee. He pushed ⎰ ⎱
one side as he set the coffee pot and cups do
way for the breakfast things. They ate in co
silence, Jen reading National Geographic
browsing his laptop, probably reading the sp
although knowing him he'd have more than one ⎰age
open, flicking back and forth between them, waiting for one
to load whilst browsing another. Always impatient.

Jen looked up at him as he typed away on the
computer, a deep frown on his face as he concentrated on
what he was doing, eyes darting back and forth. Eventually,
he slammed the lid down. 'Right, I've wasted enough time
browsing, time for a shower.'

She got up to clear the plates away but changed her
mind, sitting herself on his lap instead. She put her arms
around his neck. 'So what shall we do today? '

'Anything you like, I'm all yours,' he shrugged.

'Well,' she said, placing small kisses on his face and
neck, 'you know that chairs are only for two things, and
we've only used them for one thing so far?' She moved
position, straddling him. 'Jeez Jen, I'm spent. What's up
with you today?'

She grinned and pulled her top over her head, knowing
this would be enough to re-energise him. He was easily
aroused, 'Are you complaining?'

He lifted her body up a fraction and moved his head
down to her breasts, circling one, then the other with his
tongue. Jen threw her head back and gasped. She moved
her hands down and released him from his pyjama bottoms,
keeping a firm grip on him as she moved her hand in a slow
rhythmic motion, until she felt him tense beneath her.

'Oh God Jen, what are you doing to me?' He moved
her hand away quickly, slipped her pyjama bottoms over

lips and moved her into position on top of him. She gasped as she felt the pressure of him moving inside her.

Their movements quickly picked up pace until they were both lost in their own pleasure, gasping and moaning until they climaxed.

They remained still for a moment, but she could feel him becoming restless. He couldn't help himself. She pushed her weight down, pinning him to the spot. They both laughed, knowing what she was doing. 'That's one way of keeping me down. Maybe you should always go on top.'

She leaned back and looked at him, running her finger gently over his body. She kissed him slowly, and nuzzled his neck. She could feel him relax a little. 'You see, you do like it,' she grinned at him.

'I never said I didn't enjoy it. God, what man wouldn't enjoy a naked woman sitting on his lap in the kitchen on a Sunday morning.'

'Any woman or just me?'

'Just you, it's always you,' he smiled, kissing her.

'God, you're smarmy!' She laughed.

'And that's why you love me!'

'One of the reasons,' she corrected him.

'Would it be rude of me to go for my shower now?' he asked.

'No, you've served your purpose, for now,' she said, getting up from the chair.

'Woah Jen, give me some notice when you're going to do that. I'm still a bit, well, sensitive, you know.'

'Woose,' she said, slapping him playfully as he raced off to the shower.

'Do you want me to give you a hand?' she shouted through the bathroom door.

'I think you've given me enough of your hands in the past few hours, thanks.'

She laughed, thinking back to last night. She had enjoyed having him to herself. She loved Saturday nights spent in the flat together. She'd prepared his favourite meal and once he'd mellowed with a glass of wine, she ran herself a deep bath and filled it with aromatic oils and plenty of bubble bath. She lit a few candles and was about to get undressed when she called him through. 'Mack, can you come here a minute, I need a hand with something.'

She heard him muttering as he came through, probably irritated that he was being pulled away from his computer.

'What?' he asked rather grumpily, as he walked into the bathroom. 'Oh! Nice!' he said looking around, 'having a wee pamper session to yourself?'

'Mmmm,'

'So what do you need help with?' he looked around, puzzled. He was never one for subtleties.

She slowly undid each button on her shirt and let it drop to the floor. She was naked underneath.

'Oh!' he said, staring at her, mouth open. He was rooted to the spot.

She wriggled out of her jeans and knickers and stood before him.

'Bloody hell, so what exactly did you need a hand with?'

'I thought I might need a hand to get in the bath.'

She moved over towards him, pulled his jersey over his head and slipped her hand inside his jeans, making him groan loudly.

They lay across from each other in the bath, sipping their wine. She wasn't too bothered about actually having sex in the bath, it was too awkward and cumbersome, but

33

she enjoyed the sensual feeling of bathing together. She moved her foot up his thigh and gently massaged him with her toes. He ran his hand up her leg as far as he could reach, then reached for her hands and pulled her over towards him, so she was lying on top of him. She could taste the wine on his lips as he kissed her, moving his tongue around her mouth. He ran his hands over her back and down over her hips. She loved the feeling of their warm flesh gliding smoothly over each other, the water gently lapping around their bodies.

She could feel him hard beneath her and she rubbed her hip bone against him.

'Come on,' she whispered, getting out the bath. She wrapped herself in a warm towel, and rubbed him dry with another, before moving through to the bedroom.

'God, that's certainly one way of working up an appetite.' he said afterwards, as the lay with their legs wrapped around each other.

'That's just a little aperitif, speaking of which, I need to put the noodles on unless you want Thai curry without the carbs.'

'I'll do it. You've taken care of the starter, expertly done, I might add!' he said, planting a kiss on her lips. He pulled his jeans and jersey on and headed through to the kitchen. She took a moment to herself and wrapping the covers around her, listened to him moving about, searching for a pot, filling the kettle and pouring another wine.

She eventually got dressed and headed through to keep him company. She stood at the door, admiring him from behind. He looked sexy in his jersey, which hung loosely on his athletic frame, and faded jeans which showed off his long legs perfectly. He stood barefoot, bent over the cooker, stirring and tasting. He didn't hear her creep up behind him. She slipped her hands round his waist and lay her head on his broad back.

'I love you.'

He took a drink of his wine and turned round, grinning, 'Well, thank fuck for that, because I don't know anyone else who makes a curry this good.'

They spent the evening listening to music from their student days and reminiscing about friends and good times. Mack loved music and had a fairly extensive CD collection. He still preferred to buy CDs, although was gradually downloading music as well, succumbing to the inevitable. He jumped up and down every few moments to search through his CD collection, looking for a particular track that reminded him of something or someone. After a while, she noticed his eyes getting heavier and his head beginning to nod and jolt back quickly. It wasn't like him, but he had polished off a fair amount of wine. She noticed traces of tiredness around his eyes as she shook him gently. 'You've obviously had too much excitement for one night. Bed for you.' She turned the lights off and followed him through to bed.

He'd woken up a little by the time he'd brushed his teeth and came to bed, which was just as well, because Jen wasn't in the mood for sleeping, not yet anyway.

'I swear to God you've got the sex drive of a man,' he laughed as she pulled him on top of her and ran her hands over his broad shoulders and down his back, before slipping them inside his pyjama bottoms. 'Who says romance is dead? I still find you attractive, even wearing your PJs.'

***

They rarely slept passed eight 'o' clock at the weekend, mainly because Mack was like a cat on a hot tin roof, and couldn't settle for long. Once he was awake, he didn't stay still for long.

She felt him move towards her and slip his arm around her waist, pulling her back towards him. He gently moved his hands over her stomach and up towards her breasts, rubbing his thumb over her erect nipple. She was fully awake now and pushed her body back into his. They remained in this position, Mack behind her, and made love slowly, taking their time, making it last as long as possible.

It was the only time he ever did anything slowly. His mother had confided to her early on in their relationship that he was always on the go, although it didn't come as any surprise to Jen.

'When he was young,' his mother told her, 'he was the only one of the three who couldn't sit still. The other two would be happy painting or drawing or building lego, but not Mackenzie; he always had to be moving. Even when he was sitting, his legs were always moving, swinging back and forward or tapping away madly to some tune. It was exhausting some days. We always had to get him out and let him run off steam. Sometimes we'd take him out and the four of us would sit on the wall at the beach and just let him loose to race up and down the sand, until he would flop exhausted at our feet with a huge grin on his face. Just like an excited puppy.'

***

Her thoughts returned to the present as she poured herself another coffee and stood with her back to the kitchen sink, looking around her. It was her favourite kind of day. She could feel the heat of the sun on her skin as it shone through the large bay window in the kitchen. The skies outside were bright blue and clear, although she knew it would still be cold outside.

She loved this kitchen. It was the first room they decorated. Mack, to both his surprise and hers, turned out to be pretty handy. He had ripped out all the old kitchen units and replaced them with more modern ones, re-tiled, papered and painted. Jen had been impressed by how professional it looked. He had thrown himself into it, and had worked night and day until it was finished.

Who would have thought, when she'd met him all those years ago, that they'd be here today. They'd been together almost seven years and their relationship still felt fresh and exciting. She loved him more now than in the beginning and she found him just as sexy. She'd heard about people getting a seven year itch, but she couldn't imagine that happening to them. She could remember clearly the first time she saw him.

***

It was during fresher's week. She was out with friends at a university union bar when she spotted him. He was in the centre of a group of lads, who all seemed to be talking at once, competing for attention. Mack was just standing, nodding and smiling occasionally, but didn't seem too bothered about taking part in the conversation. He looked slightly bored if anything. She watched him from a spot at the bar. He was good looking, tall, broad, a very sporty physique. He had a thick mop of messy dark hair which was just crying out for someone to run their hands through it.

He glanced over and smiled. She gave a short smile back and turned back towards her friends, accepting another drink, which she downed quickly, before they headed off to another bar.

It was a good few months later when they ran into each other again, literally. She was heading out of a club one Saturday night when some drunk student bumped into her, knocking her off her balance. She felt a strong hand grab her around the waist, stopping her from falling.

'Woah, got ya.'

She turned around and was face-to-face with him. His face was no more than a few inches from her own. His dark brown eyes shone as he grinned at her, revealing his perfect teeth. She could detect a faint smell of soap and possibly aftershave. It was subtle and pleasant, not overpowering like some of the guys she knew.

'I.... thanks.' She smiled back at him.

'No problems. Saved you from a potentially embarrassing situation there, although I'm surprised you can stand upright in those heels,' he said looking down at her feet and catching a glimpse of her slim calves. 'Nice though,' he said raising an eyebrow.

'Thanks. What would you suggest I wear when out dancing? A nice pair of brogues?'

'I've no idea what they are, but I'm sure you'd look good in them.'

'Ha, you really don't know what they look like, do you?'

He held out his hand, 'Mack. I don't normally come out with such cheesy lines. You just caught me unawares.'

'Wasn't it the other way around?' she laughed. 'I'm Jen, nice to meet you Mack.'

'Were you heading out?'

'Mmm, just for fresh air. My friends are still in there.'

'So what are you doing in a hell hole like this then?'

'Oh I went with the majority vote. I haven't been here before so had no expectations. What about you? Are you a regular here?'

'Nah, not really, I just fancied a drink so ended up here with the hard-core clubbers.'

They chatted for a while until he noticed her shivering, not surprisingly, as they were standing by the door and she was wearing a short, figure hugging dress, with spaghetti straps and nothing to cover her shoulders.

'Here,' he said, placing his hoodie round her shoulders, 'You look frozen.'

He stepped back and cast a critical eye over her, 'not bad, it adds a certain something to the ensemble.'

'Let me guess, you're studying Art and Design,' she laughed.

'If only! It'd be more interesting than maths. God, I wish I wasn't so gallant! I'm bloody freezing. Look, wait here, promise you won't run away.'

'I wouldn't run off with your favourite hoodie now would I?'

He disappeared and came back wearing a padded jacket. 'That's better,' he said zipping it up to his neck. 'Might not look all that attractive, but it does the job.'

'Oh, that looks so much warmer this this,' she said, nodding at the hoodie. 'Swap?'

'Awe, jeez, how can I say no? Alternatively, how about we get out of here and find somewhere warmer?'

'Mmm, like where? I'm not sure what you're suggesting.'

'Oh, nothing like that! Maybe just head to the club along the road. It plays decent music, and I know the guy on the door. He'll let us jump the queue. Just thought a dance would heat us up.'

'Well, put like that, how can I resist? Lead the way.'

The club was much better, as promised. They danced, chatted and danced some more. She hadn't met anyone this easy to get on with in a long time. Most guys she met were either quite nervous around her or trying too hard to impress, which just put her off. Mack was the opposite. He seemed pretty relaxed and spoke to her as if she imagined he'd speak to any of his friends or family. He wasn't obviously trying to hit on her, although she could tell he was interested. They flirted playfully with each other most of the night.

As the night drew to a close, he suggested they share a taxi. 'I'm pretty sure you won't be able to walk home in those shoes, although I must admit, you've done a pretty good job of dancing in them. My mate's a taxi driver. I'll give him a call and see if he's in the area. I really can't face walking to the taxi rank and waiting around for ages.'

'Is there anyone you don't know?' she smiled.

'To be honest, I've played my full hand already. These are my two most useful mates. We play football together, that's how I know them. All my other friends are just students.'

They arranged to meet the taxi a street away from the club, to prevent anyone else taking it.

'He said he'll be about five minutes,' Mack said to her. 'Now, I was thinking, to save any awkwardness or embarrassment in the taxi, maybe I should ask you for your number now. In fact, do you fancy meeting up again?'

'Yes, that would be great.'

'Brilliant. How about coffee tomorrow afternoon?'

'That quick! Erm, yes that should be fine.'

Mack typed her number into his phone and immediately texted her so she had his number. She opened it and saved it to her contacts, 'Great,' she smiled up at him.

'Now, the other thing before the taxi comes, I know you're probably going to ask me in for a coffee when we arrive at yours, and you'll be hoping that we'll skip the coffee and yet just get straight to the interesting stuff, but to save you the embarrassment, I'll just let you know up front, I'm not that type of guy. Never on a first date. I have my reputation and integrity to think about.'

Jen laughed. He grinned at her, 'I don't normally kiss on a first date either, however, given these are exceptional circumstances and it's a race against time before Pete gets here, I'd say I have to act completely out of character and kiss you.' He reached down and kissed her before she could reply or protest, not that she had any plans for the latter.

She opened her mouth to say something when the sound of a horn made them both jump. Pete the taxi driver was here and grinning out at them, obviously having witnessed their first kiss. As much as she was disappointed he'd arrived when he did, she was also very grateful. It was late, she was cold and her feet were aching, although she daren't admit it. She gave Pete her address and they headed across the city to student land. It was no more than fifteen minutes as the streets were quiet and Pete drove like a typical taxi driver. She insisted on giving Mack some money and jumped out of the taxi before there was an awkward moment.

'See you tomorrow,' she said, kissing him lightly on the cheek before getting out of the taxi.

'You smarmy git. How did you land a bird like that?' Pete asked.

'You're pure class Pete! Rule number one, never refer to the love of your life as a bird. Now drive on my man.'

She did in fact meet him for coffee the next day and from there they were pretty much inseparable. They did spend time apart of course, but gradually the time spent apart grew less and less, until eventually nobody could remember a time when they weren't together, and whenever Mack's name was mentioned, Jen's would follow and vice versa. She did often feel they had the perfect charmed life. They sailed through University, both got jobs in Edinburgh and eventually managed to buy the flat in an area they loved. Then he proposed to her and now they were going to get married! How perfect was that? Even the wedding preparations hadn't been too stressful so far, although admittedly they hadn't really done much.

She got a nervous, excited feeling in the pit of her stomach whenever she thought about it. She couldn't wait, and she knew that on the day, she'd be more excited than nervous. They had an idea about where they wanted to get married and when, all they had to do now was get round to booking it. She had chosen and ordered her dress and was hoping to look for bridesmaids' dresses next weekend, and once that was sorted, she thought the rest would just gradually fall into place. She had hoped to persuade Mack to visit a few potential venues this afternoon if he was in the mood. Her plan was to find a walk they could do near one of the venues, so they'd both be happy.

She heard him come out of the shower and head to the bedroom to get changed. By the time she'd made him a fresh coffee he was sitting in the lounge, browsing on the i-pad. She was on her way to the shower when she heard the front door bell ring. The keys were never anywhere to be found. Mack didn't like hanging them up in the hall in case

42

they were burgled, so she rummaged through her bag, knowing they were there somewhere. She shouted through her apologies to whoever was at the front door, mildly curious as to who it could be at this time of the morning, but sure it was probably their elderly neighbor, who frequently called round with various bits of important information.

Chapter 3
Mack

'What do you mean, you've split up?' his father asked him in astonishment.

His mother came and sat next to him on the sofa, with a look of both concern and disbelief on her face. 'I can't believe it! What on earth has happened? You two were so...'

He put his hand up to stop her, shaking his head, 'I know, I know what we were, but it's over.'

'How can it be over, just like that? Are you sure?'

'Yes, of course I'm sure. I couldn't be more sure!' he snapped.

'What your mother means,' his father interjected, 'is, are you sure that it's not just, well, just a silly misunderstanding or something that's been said in the heat of the moment. You know it wouldn't be the first time an argument gets out of hand and neither side can back down. Perhaps things have been said which weren't meant and it seems like there's no way back, but I'm sure it's just a a heat of the moment thing. You probably just need to sleep on it and it'll all seem a lot better in the morning.'

Mack shook his head and stared at the floor. How could he begin to explain it to them?

'I... I take it Jen's at the flat?' his mother hesitated, wary of saying the wrong thing.

He looked up, confused. 'Yes, why?'

'Oh, no real reason, I just wondered... I'll make up the bed for you in your old room and you can stay for as long as you like, or need.'

He nodded, staring at the floor again, 'thanks mum.'

His father sat next to him and gave him an awkward pat on the knee. 'Can I get you anything? Whiskey?'

'No, no thanks dad. I think I'll just head up if that's Ok,'

'Of course, maybe that's best,' he said, almost too quickly, his relief difficult to conceal.

Mack walked into his old room just as his mother was smoothing down the sheets. She gave a weak smile and hesitated before moving towards him. She placed a hand lightly on his shoulder but pulled him into a hug as she noticed his head drop and his shoulders begin to shake. She stroked the back of his head as she had done when he was a small boy and in need of comfort as he wept onto her shoulder.

'Sorry, sorry,' he said, pulling away from her, wiping his eyes, embarrassed. He couldn't remember the last time he'd cried but he knew he'd been a child.

'Shhh, don't apologise,' she said, sitting him down on the bed. 'You're never too old to cry. You're hurting, it's natural.' They sat in silence for a moment, only the sound of his sniffing breaking the quiet.

'Have you really no idea why you've split up?'

He shook his head, 'Don't ask mum, I can't....,' he broke off, his voice trembling.

45

'Ok, let's leave it just now. The best thing you can do just now is get some rest. You probably won't get much sleep, but try and rest. I'll be here when... if you need me.'

'Thanks mum,' he said curling up into a ball on his bed. His mother closed the door quietly behind her, leaving him alone in his room. He had a tight knot o his stomach and his heart felt as if it was made of lead.

He took some comfort from the familiar surroundings of his room, which didn't seem to have changed from the day he left. He looked around and was touched to think his mother had kept it exactly the same. You hear about parents redecorating their child's room the moment they leave home, but not his parents, or his mother in particular. He could imagine her putting her foot down and insisting the room stayed the same.

He looked at the shelf on the opposite wall. Still filled with trophies and medals he'd won. He spotted a large trophy in the shape of a golden boot and remembered how proud his parents had been when he'd been presented with it for player of the year, voted for by his fellow football team mates. He'd been eleven. He lay there in the dark, feeling lonely and ashamed, wishing he was eleven again.

He'd fully intended to tell his parents the truth, but when it came to it, he couldn't bring himself to do it. He knew they'd be disappointed to say the least, but it would be so much worse than that. They'd be totally ashamed of him, furious and humiliated by his behaviour. He didn't know if he could bear to hurt them, but equally, he owed it to Jen to own up and be a man, otherwise they'd blame her and she didn't deserve that.

His father would be particularly furious. He loved Jen as if she was his own and was delighted when they announced their engagement. He never tired of telling

Mack how lucky he was and how he needed to be sure and do the best by her. Mack groaned inwardly, recollecting all the conversations they'd had over the years.

His father and Jen's father were both keen golfers and became good friends and golf buddies. How could they possibly remain friends now? When he thought about Jen's parents, the knot in his stomach tightened further.

How the hell was he going to explain this? He couldn't explain it to himself, let alone justify it. There was no justification for what he'd done. Even in the midst of seeing Abbi, he had no idea of why he was doing it. He wasn't really the type of guy to have lots of women on the go. He wasn't even a big flirt. He'd always felt slightly superior to the other guys he knew who who felt compelled to flirt with every woman they came into contact with, or those who had problems when it came to monogamous relationships. He realised now that he was no better than them and that hurt He wasn't squeaky clean and he suspected Jen wasn't either. He wasn't blind to a pretty woman and they had often joked about other people they fancied or if they weren't with each other, who, out of their friends, would they be with. A dangerous game to some, but they both knew there was no harm in it. They were so strong together and never doubted each other's commitment. Jen could have had a crush on his best friend and he would never have felt in the least bit threatened. And likewise, until now, he was sure Jen would have felt the same.

So why did he take things further with Abbi? He cast his mind back to that fateful night. Not the very first night he met her at the bus stop, because as much as he had been attracted to her that night, he hadn't taken it any further, despite knowing he could have. He knew she was interested but equally, he knew there was no question of taking it

47

further. So what had changed in the time between that first meeting and their second?

Nothing! He honestly didn't think that anything had changed. He still loved Jen. True, they now lived together, but he didn't recall ever feeling unhappy about that or that it had changed things. He didn't feel trapped or under the thumb as some of his friends suggested he might. He'd proposed to her a year after they moved in together and had never been happier. Jen never put any pressure or demands on him. She was a strong character, but he had no problem with that. It was one of the reasons he loved her.

It was probably nothing about his relationship with Jen that was the trigger, but something about Abbi that attracted him. She seemed more vulnerable, less confident than Jen and perhaps he'd been drawn by a need to protect her and look after her. He had never really needed to look after Jen as such, not outwardly anyway. She loved to be loved and wanted, but that was different from needing it. Abbi seemed less sure of herself, uncertain and hesitant and he had felt a strong desire to make her happy.

He had a restless night, drifting in and out of sleep. Eventually, at five 'o' clock, he decided there was no point in trying to sleep any longer. It was never going to happen. His eyes, red and puffy, stinging from tiredness and tears. He made his way quietly downstairs, not wanting to wake anyone as he was in no mood for company.

He checked himself in the hall mirror. *Jesus Christ, I look a wreck.* How the hell was he going to get through the day feeling like this? He thought about calling in sick but decided against it. The last thing he wanted to do was hang around here all day with his parents questioning him. No, he'd be better to go to work and tell the Head he wasn't feeling great, which would explain any under-performance

48

and get him out of any extracurricular activities which he was often asked to do. He had one change of clothes, which were a bit casual, but would have to do. He made himself a strong coffee and sat down at the kitchen table, putting his head in his hands as he closed his eyes. He was trying to make some sense of what he'd done but it was no use. He had no idea why he started up a relationship with someone else, but it was all his own doing and he knew he'd need to face up to it. Just maybe not today.

Miraculously, he made it through the day, albeit at fifty percent his usual level, although Mack's fifty percent was most other people's one hundred percent. A few of his cheekier pupils commented on his shabby appearance and bleary eyes. The Head was understanding and told him to do what he could, but they'd manage to get cover if necessary. This only served to heighten his guilt. Everyone was being extra nice to him. If only they knew what he'd done.

He wasn't sure if he should try to contact Jen. He checked his phone surreptitiously under the desk as often as he could, but there was no message. What did he expect? If nothing else, he needed to get some clothes, but ultimately, he'd rather go back and try to work it out, although after the scene yesterday, that was highly unlikely.

***

What the hell had Abbi been thinking of, coming to the flat? He knew the answer to that question of course. The moment he saw her standing outside the door, he knew everything was over. His whole body froze momentarily, before the adrenalin kicked in and he found himself racing for the front door, knowing it was too late, but what was the alternative?

He saw Jen, smiling at first, then faltering. It didn't take more than a few seconds for her to realise what was going on. Mack's face gave it all away.

'Go inside,' he told her, 'I'll deal with this, I know what it's all about.' He tried to push her back and close the front door behind him, but Jen wedged it open.

Mack looked desperate. 'Ok, look,' he said frantically, 'can we all come inside? Let's not do this on the street.'

Jen blocked the way. She had a cold hard look on her face. 'You're not setting a foot inside this flat,' she said to Abbi. Turning to Mack, she said, 'and neither are you unless you have one helluva good explanation for all this but I seriously doubt it.'

Mack hadn't known what to say, and in those crucial moments that followed, he'd said nothing. Perhaps if he had, there would have been some chance of salvaging things, but the silence said it all.

Jen slammed the door, locking and bolting it, making sure he couldn't get back in.

He remembers looking helplessly at Abbi, then felt the anger rising inside him. He turned on her. 'Abbi, what the fuck are you doing here, what are you thinking of? How the hell did you know where I live?'

'I followed you,' she said quietly.

'You... wha...?' he faltered. 'followed me? How, when?' He'd moved away from the front door by now and was standing at the gate. The front door flew open and Jen hurtled a bag out towards him and slammed the door closed again. Mack stood there, looking lost and helpless. He turned back to Abbi.

50

'I saw you both together yesterday, holding hands.' Mack could see the pain in her eyes. She was struggling to stay in control. Mack knew why.

'You lied to me,' she said matter-of-factly. 'You didn't look like a couple on the verge of splitting up. You were laughing together. You put your arm around her shoulders and kissed her. I couldn't see her properly, but I assumed it was Jen, unless you've got a whole harem of us on the go.'

He shook his head and stared at his shoes. He couldn't look her in the eye. He hadn't actually lied to her as such, just hadn't told her the truth. He couldn't think of what to say when she confronted him all those months ago, asking exactly *when* Mack was going to leave. She was never in any doubt that it would happen, it was just a matter of when. He had told her he and Jen were still living together, but was vague about how things were between them, so his silence and lack of explanation had perhaps led Abbi to believe that the relationship was over or at least in trouble. He had often looked back and wondered why the hell he'd let her carry on believing that. Abbi's confrontation was a perfect opportunity to end it all and walk away without anyone finding out, but stupidly, he'd carried on with the whole thing. He could have saved everyone a whole lot of hurt, but at that time, there was still a part of him that wasn't ready to give her up. Even now, looking at her, he still had feelings for her, although the fury he felt at her for following him and turning up here superseded anything else. He knew he had no right to feel angry, but he did.

He reached out his hand towards her. 'Look, Abbi...'

'Don't touch me!' she spat.

He recoiled. This was a side of her he hadn't seen, and shouldn't have come as a surprise to him, but it did somehow.

51

'I could *almost* have forgiven you if you had meant to leave her,' she spat, 'but I see now that you had no intention of splitting up with her, did you?. I told myself *these things happen*, and *no one's to blame, it's just unfortunate circumstances*. But I was fooling myself. I still can't believe you could be so deceitful. It's, it's.... a side of you I just don't recognise. I feel everything we had has been one big lie. You're not the person I fell in love with. I'm such an idiot. You've made such a fool out of me.'

Mack could feel her pain. It was his pain as well. He truly hadn't meant any of this to happen. It was only now that it became clear that he was messing with other people's feelings. He hadn't realised he had this huge capacity to hurt others in this way. How could he not have known this?

He reached again, but drew his hand back. 'Abbi, I'm so sorry, I...'

'Save it Mack. We have nothing more to say to each other. You've already humiliated me enough without adding to it with pathetic excuses and more lies. You've destroyed something in me today and nothing you say will ever reverse that.'

She turned and walked away. Her head was bowed and Mack knew she was crying. He sat on the garden wall staring into space. He had no idea how long he'd been sitting there but the cold stone began to bite into his flesh. It was a warm day, but he felt chilled to the bone. He turned and looked at the flat behind him, half expecting to see Jen at the window, but of course there was no sign of her. In fact, there was no sign of life in there at all. She was probably through in one of the back rooms, as far away from him as possible.

He picked up the bag she had thrown out at him. Some clothes, a jacket, his phone and car keys, and at the bottom of the bag, her engagement ring. He rolled it around between his thumb and forefinger before putting it in his pocket.

He was at a total loss for what to do next. His whole body felt heavy and numb, unable to move. Slowly, he made his way to the car and sat there with his head on the steering wheel for a while. A knock at the passenger window made him jump. It was Mrs. Watson from next door, looking concerned. He groaned inwardly, but tried to smile. She was lovely, but boy could she talk and there was no doubt this morning's drama wouldn't have escaped her.

He rolled the window down, 'morning, how are you?' he asked politely.

'Oh, so-so, you know. Waiting on this damn hip operation so I can get going again. It's been four months now, so much for the great NHS, still I can't really complain. I've been pretty lucky to get to this age without being in too much need of it. But I'm not here to chat about me. You don't look too good. Had a little tiff have you? You know it's funny, I was just saying to Isla up the road that I've never seen you two argue, but it looks like I might have been wrong. Don't worry about it, everybody has fall outs you know, lord knows James and I had a fair few arguments over the years, but it's natural. You'll get over it and wonder what all the fuss was about.'

He was watching her lips move and wondered if they would ever stop. He had no idea what she was saying but nodded, hopefully in all the right places. He was glancing over her shoulder for any sign of Jen. Mrs Watson drew breath and was about to go again when he interjected.

'Thanks, I appreciate what you're saying. I think I need to go and clear my head and give Jen some space though,' he said starting up the engine and putting the car into gear. 'I'll see you later, Ok?' he said as the window slowly closed on her.

He checked his mirrors and drove off. He had no idea where he was going but he needed to get away from the flat.

He drove to the beach and sat there for a while, then to Arthur's Seat, where he sat staring out over the city. It was getting dark and he was cold and tired. He had no idea whether he should contact Jen or not. He felt he should make some contact and he desperately wanted to speak to her, but knew it was unlikely that she'd want to speak to him at all. Maybe he should leave it and give her space, but then perhaps she'd be hurt and angry that he hadn't even tried to get in touch. He must have reached for his phone a hundred times, checking it, starting texts then discarding them.

He had absolutely no idea what to do. He felt lost and helpless and for the first time in a long time, really needed his mother. It was at that point he felt his eyes prickle with tears. He headed home, but drove as slowly as he could. This wasn't a conversation he was looking forward to. In the end he didn't own up. He couldn't, not yet.

***

The next few days were some of the worst. Abbi sent a text to say his belongings were in a bag in the wheelie bin and the refuse would be collected on Thursday. It was up to him whether he wanted to go and retrieve it. He couldn't face rummaging through the bin like some sad homeless person.

Jen hadn't been in touch. In the end he texted her. *Jen, I'm so sorry. I know these words seem trivial and meaningless but there are no words to portray how sorry I really feel and what an idiot I am. Can we meet, please? M xx*

She replied the next day. *I'll be out the flat tomorrow until eight. Please come by and collect whatever you need or want. After that I'm changing the locks and then will put the flat on the market. Please don't wait for me to come home tomorrow. This will be the last time I ever contact you directly.'*

He stared at the text for ages. He was gutted. He knew she would be mad and hurt, but he truly hadn't expected this. He knew Jen had always said she would throw him out if he ever had an affair and there would be no second chances, but he still thought that in the cold light of day, they would have both given each other another chance.

With a heavy heart, he went round to the flat and collected a few things. He took all his clothes and personal belongings and a few photos. He left a note saying what he'd taken and that if she wanted these back, it was no problem. He wrote a letter three times, trying to apologise, explain, beg. But he ripped them all up. Eventually, he left about seven thirty. If he was honest, he actually couldn't bear to see her or to look at her.

***

The truth came out a week after Mack had returned to his parents. He hadn't realised living at home would be so stifling. His parents were always there, no matter which

55

way he turned. He knew they meant well, but he felt they were always hovering at his shoulder, probing and cajoling. He couldn't bear the looks that passed between them. His father, in particular, was becoming unbearable. Several times a day he asked if Jen had been in touch, until Mack eventually snapped.

'For God's sake, no she bloody hasn't. Do you think I'd still be here if she had?'

'Well bloody well get in touch with her then for all our sakes, Mack,' his father bellowed back at him.

'No, I can't OK?'

'Why not? I'll be damned if I'm going to stand by and see you lose her because of your pig headed stubbornness! Why the hell can't you pick up the phone, and I mean actually make a call, none of this bloody texting nonsense, and speak to the Goddamn girl,' his fathered shouted.

'Because it's all my fault. There's no way she'll take me back. She's putting the flat on the market for fuck's sake.'

His parents looked shocked. He wasn't sure if it was the language or Jen selling the flat. Probably both.

In the end he just came out with it. 'I cheated on her. It's all my fault.' He hung his head and waited for the fallout.

His mother dropped to the sofa. 'Oh Mack,' she whispered.

His father, as predicted was more vocal. 'WHAT? Did I just hear you right? You… you cheated on her? Mack, what the bloody hell were you thinking of? Why?'

Mack shook his head.

'Well bloody well answer me man. Why?'

'I don't know! OK?' he shouted back, 'I have absolutely no idea. Jesus Christ I wish I knew, but I don't. I've totally fucked everything up and it's all my fault.'

'I just can't believe you could do such a thing. What was going through your mind? How could you, to someone like Jen? Have you any idea what that will do to her?' he yelled.

That was enough for Mack. He knew what he'd done was inexcusable, but coming from his father, it was hard to take.

'I don't know dad,' he yelled back, 'why don't you tell me how it will make her feel? Why don't you tell me how I could do such a thing? Let's hear it straight from the horse's mouth shall we?'

'How dare you speak to me like that.' His father's fury was tangible, but it wasn't enough to stop Mack. They squared up to each other, neither going to be the one to back down first. The sound of quiet sobs from the sofa made them both stop. His mother was dabbing tears from her eyes.

'Now look what you've done,' his father glared at him, 'you've upset your mother. This isn't about me or what I did, this is about you and the sooner you face up to it like a man the better. Don't try to deflect this situation by pulling me into it. I apologized all those years ago and your mother had the good grace to accept it and we moved on.'

'Well bully for you. You said sorry and that was it. It doesn't make it any better though does it? Do you think mum was any less hurt than Jen? What makes what you did any different or more acceptable than what I've just done? Really dad, you make me sick! You can't see how ridiculous you are standing there lecturing me can you?'

'The circumstances were different,' he said coldly.

57

'Yeah, you had kids. I don't! I would say that's worse, wouldn't you?' Mack spat back at him.

'I know what I did was wrong. I know I hurt all of you, which is why I hoped you'd never repeat my mistakes.'

Mack watched as his father left the room. He sat next to his mother and took her hand. 'Sorry mum, for what I've done and for raking all that up. You didn't deserve to be party to all of that.'

The next few days were spent tiptoeing around his parents, trying to avoid contact with them as much as possible.

***

A welcome text came from his school friend Josh. *Aye, aye, a wee bird tells me someone's been a bit of a naughty boy. Am thinking you might be in need of a drink. Fancy a pint at the Teuchtar Arms?*

Mack replied immediately, *you don't know how much I need a pint mate*. It was Friday and he couldn't face football training, which was completely out of character.

'So,' Josh asked, taking a thirst quenching gulp of his lager before continuing, 'I'm guessing it must be bad by the look of you,' he said, matter of factly.

Mack nodded, adjusting the beer mat before placing his glass down. He'd drunk half already.

'She must have been some woman, to tempt you away from Jen. What were you thinking about? I mean *Jen* for God's sake. Most men I know would give their eye teeth to have somebody like her, and you, you cocky bastard, not content with that, go and shag somebody else at the same time!'

'I Know. Fuck it, I've been such an idiot. Have you ever done anything so stupid and you don't even know why?'

'Yep, but nothing on this scale.' There was an awkward break in the conversation. It seemed Mack wasn't much for talking. 'So… who was she? Was it just a one-night stand?'

'No, that's the thing, it wasn't just a one night stand. I've been seeing her for a few months.' Mack knew it was more like a year but he couldn't own up to this, even to himself.

'Months? Jesus man. When? How? Did anyone else know?' he asked, trying to hide the note of petulance which had crept into his voice. He would be put out if Mack had confided in someone else before him.

'No, no one else knew and God knows how I managed to keep it from everyone, especially Jen, although Abbi didn't know until just a few months ago.'

'YOU ARE JOKING!' he stated in disbelief, 'you mean… she didn't know you were engaged to Jen?'

'No, she didn't know anything about Jen.'

'God Mack, this is getting worse by the minute. Who was she?'

He sighed, his shoulders dropping, 'Just someone I met at a party.'

'A party? What just some random person? What possessed you to start some *random* when you had everything with Jen? I mean, I could just about understand it if it had been someone you'd known for a while and had…you know… developed feelings for, but someone you just met.' He said more to himself than to Mack.

'Cheers Josh, thanks for stating the obvious and making me feel worse than I thought I could.'

'Sorry man, but I just don't get it,' he said, running his hands through his hair and taking another gulp of his pint. 'What made you follow through with someone you just met? She must have made a fairly big impression on you to make you go chasing after her when you had Jen waiting at home on you. I mean, you've always said you were a lucky bastard to land someone like Jen, what the hell is this other bird like?'

'Well, she's not a *bird*, and yeah, she did make an impression on me. I don't know, I can't expect you to understand, God knows, I hardly understand it myself, but there was just something about her.'

'Were you and Jen having... you know... problems?'

Mack shook his head, 'I wish in some ways we were. It would have made more sense of it all.'

'So what did Jen say?'

Mack shrugged, 'What do you think? Actually, to be honest she didn't *say* anything, she threw me out and wouldn't answer my calls or text. She told me to go and collect my things, and that was that.'

'Woah, she must be mad. What are you going to do? Will you try to get her back?'

'No, not just now. She's made it clear that she wants nothing to do with me. And she's not mad, she's totally devastated. She's selling the flat.'

'Selling the flat? God that's a bit quick.'

'I know. I can't help thinking she's being a bit rash, but I wouldn't even dare speak to her about it.'

Josh nodded his head in agreement, 'No, you're right. I think you're on thin ground already. I wouldn't go in there with any suggestions or opinions. God, do you think that it's really over, I can't believe it. You two were always so solid. The really irritating *golden couple*, although what was more irritating was that you were both so bloody nice. This will put a few smiles on some folk's faces though.'

'Thanks!' Mack said sarcastically, 'and yeah, it feels like it's over, but I really hope not. All I want is a chance to meet her, although God knows what I'd say. I can't really explain it.'

'And what about the other one, this Abbi? Where is she in all this?'

'What do you think? That's over as well. And before you say it, yes, I've truly fucked up, I've lost them both.'

Josh exhaled loudly. 'Man, that's tough. My shout, same again?' he drained his drink and nodded in the direction of Mack's empty glass.

When he returned he looked at Mack with a puzzled expression. 'So, tell me to mind my own business if you like, but did you like her then, this Abbi?'

'Yeah, I did, do. God it's such a tangled mess. I didn't know it was possible to like two people equally at the same time and the thing that's cutting me up is that I've lost both of them.'

'If you had to choose between them, who would it be?'

Mack shook his head. 'I can't answer that. Even if I knew the answer, I don't think I could say.'

'You see, the way I see it is that you've never had to work at anything before. Everything just slips into place for you, you're one of life's lucky bastards. Whatever you want, you get, including Jen. I mean let's face it, you never really had to work hard to get her did you? She just fell into your lap.'

Mack had a sudden vision of Jen sitting on his lap last Sunday and had to shake himself to regain his concentration.

'If you did have to work for Jen, then you'd have appreciated her more and wouldn't have been so tempted to stray.'

'A right Sigmund Freud you are. When did you get your degree in Psychology?'

'It's not rocket science as they say. It stands to reason, if you hadn't have had Jen eating out of the palm of your hand, then you wouldn't have been as likely to stray.'

'Maybe, but can you stop talking about her being in my lap and eating out of my hand? It's a bit too raw.'

'Oh, yeah, sorry man. Well, put it another way, if someone just came along and handed you a Ferrari, you'd love it for a bit but would probably start taking it for granted and if it got a bit dented and scratched along the way, well, it maybe wouldn't hurt as much as if you'd paid for it out of your hard earned cash. Maybe you wouldn't even take as good care of it as if you'd had to save up for it and wait for it for a while. In other words, if you'd saved for it and waited for it and bought it out of your own money, then you would love it and look after it like it was the most precious thing in your life. So, what I'm saying is...'

'Yeah, yeah, I get it.'

'No but that's just the half of it, hear me out. Let's say that someone then comes along and gives you a Maserati, say, without you even asking for it, then man, you've got two beauties, and now you're feeling like a right cocky bastard and you don't appreciate either of them.'

'Yeah, right, I get it OK, now enough with the car analogies, although, whilst we're using the car analogy, consider this. You have two high class sports cars, obviously you like them both but you're only allowed to keep one. Which one do you choose and why?'

Josh took a large gulp of his beer and placed the glass slowly back down on the beer mat, considering the answer carefully. 'Good question, but it's simple. You go with your gut feeling. Not what you think you should do, but with the one which gives you most pleasure. The one that you wake up thinking about in the morning. So, which one gives you most pleasure?' he said with a smirk.

'Steady,'

'Which one is the best ri…?'

'Stop right there! I know where you're headed. If we're still talking about cars, then the Ferrari every time.'

'Really? It would be the Maserati for me. Classy, rare, expensive and a very smooth ride I believe.'

'No, the Ferrari is a classic, understated, not gauche and in your face like a Maserati.'

'Mmm, so which one is the Ferrari and which is the Maserati?'

'I've no idea,' Mack sighed, 'if only it were that simple, in all honesty, I don't think I have the luxury of having a choice. I think I'll need to hand them both back to the kind person who gifted them to me, although it'll be hard to move on from a Ferrari or Maserati.'

'Welcome to the real world mate.' Josh finished his beer and held up his glass, 'another one here and then we can go and find ourselves a couple of Ford Fiestas.'

Mack laughed, 'thanks, but no thanks.'

Mack and Josh said their goodbyes and Mack headed off in search of somewhere still serving drink.

***

It was mid-afternoon when he finally woke up properly. He felt a wreck. He was badly in need of food and drink but didn't think he could face going downstairs in this state and doing the walk of shame across the kitchen floor with his parents looking on in disbelief.

As if reading his thoughts, there was a gentle knock on the door and his mother poked her head around it.

'Thought you might be in need of this,' she said, holding up a cup of tea in front of her.

He mustered a smile and pulled himself up to a sitting position. She sat on the edge of the bed, 'mind if I join you?'

'Is that a rhetorical question?' he asked sarcastically.

'You're in no position to be cheeky,' she nudged him, sitting down anyway, and stretching her long slim legs out on top of the bed.

'Owe, careful, I'm a bit delicate.'

'Oh, I nearly forgot, I brought you these,' she said, fishing two paracetamol out of her pocket.

He looked up at her sheepishly, 'thanks.'

'It can't be easy for you staying here. It's bad enough you've lost Jen, but having to stay here as well. It must feel a bit claustrophobic.'

'No, it's fine, really.'

'Liar. I can tell by the look on your face that it's not fine. You were never any good at hiding your feelings.' She rubbed his hair affectionately.

He pulled away from her, smiling 'Owe that hurts. Hangover, remember? Do you think I have lost her?' he asked tentatively.

'Mmm. It's not looking good from where I'm sitting. What do you think?'

He shrugged and sighed. 'I hope not. How's dad?' he asked after a pause.

'Angry, hurt, stubborn,' she smiled. 'for what it's worth, I think he was a bit hypocritical giving you such a hard time, but he meant it with good reason. I think he hoped you would all learn by his mistakes rather than follow in his footsteps.'

'Sorry, I said some awful things, and I know I've done wrong, but I just saw red, when he of all people, started having a go at me.'

She sighed, 'you know, I haven't really told anyone this, but I didn't blame your father entirely for what happened.'

Mack turned and stared at her, not quite believing his ears. 'Mum! Please don't tell me you think you were in any way to blame.'

'No, not to blame exactly, but I sort of understood why he'd done it, in a warped sort of way. I suspected way before he admitted it actually.'

'Jesus mum, you suspected? How long did you let it go on for before you did anything?'

'Oh not long, six months maybe.'

'Six months! Bloody hell! What were you thinking?'

'What were you thinking?' she blurted out before she could stop herself. 'Sorry,' she said as she saw his hurt expression. She sighed, 'it's hard to explain and probably harder for you to understand, but when you have children, your attention focuses entirely on them. It has to. And you have less time for each other. By the time you have three children, any thought of focusing on each other goes entirely. In fact, you can't remember what life was like before, and you'd probably struggle to converse at all if you did find each other alone together. By the time your father and I were alone together we were so tired or grumpy or both, that conversation was poor. I'm not saying we didn't love each other or our relationship was under threat, just that it had changed. So in some ways, when I began to suspect he was seeing someone else, it didn't surprise me, and in fact, and this is the part I haven't confessed to anyone, a small part of me was relieved.'

Mack frowned, clearly confused.

'You see for a while at least, it took the pressure off me. I had one less person to think about and in actual fact, things improved between us for a short while. Your father seemed happier and I didn't have this huge guilt hanging over me.'

'Guilt! What did you have to feel guilty about?'

'Guilt that I had no time for him. Guilt that I couldn't be bothered.' She cast Mack a sideways glance. 'Is that an awful thing to say?'

'No, not really.'

'You're lying again. I know it's an awful thing to say about your own husband, but sadly, that's the way I felt at the time. Anyway, eventually your father's guilt got the better of him and he ended it with her, but not before some damage had been done. I began to resent the fact that he was having an affair. He was out enjoying himself while I was at home looking after three young children. I was shattered and almost in tears at the end of every day with exhaustion, and he would saunter in, looking lively and happy. I confronted him, and well… you know the rest.'

Mack took her hand. 'God mum that must have been awful for you. I didn't realise having kids was so difficult.'

'It's not,' she laughed, 'I wouldn't change it for the world, apart from your father having the affair that is.'

'I see what you're trying to say, but even so, couples all over the world over have kids and not all men go off and have an affair because their wives spend more time looking

66

after the baby rather than them. I think your loyalties are misguided.'

'Oh do you now? Well, I know you might find it hard to understand, but the fact that we had a family, three young children, meant that we had to deal with things differently. I put my children first and took him back. Gave him a second chance because I couldn't bear the thought of you growing up without him or him without you. That would have destroyed him.'

Mack groaned, 'Oh God, please don't say you did it for us. That makes me feel awful.'

'No! I didn't mean it like that. I did do it for the sake of the three of you, but only because I could see how remorseful he felt. I knew he'd never do it again and for the sake of you I gave him a second chance. Maybe if we hadn't had children I would have had the luxury of telling him to sling his hook and never darken my doorstep again, but that wasn't the case, and my desire for us to be a family was stronger than my pride I guess. It was a no brainer as you would say.'

'Yeah, but was it worth it for a life of unhappiness?'

'I'm not unhappy! I've been really happy with your father and you three apart from that one mishap. So you see, it was worth me giving him a second chance. I'm glad I did.'

'I was thanking my lucky stars Jen and I don't have children, but maybe I'd have more chance of a reconciliation if we did.'

'No, to be honest, if you do get back together, then you'll know it's because you love each other and she's forgiven you because she wants to and nothing to do with children.'

'Yeah, I guess.'

67

'I know you won't thank me for saying this, but you can no longer hold yourself in higher esteem than your father. You don't have the upper hand anymore.'

Mack hung his head. 'Holy Fuck!'

'And I'll remind you that you're in my house. You can save that language for the football field.'

'Sorry. But God, it's bad enough that I've lost Jen, but this as well, on top of the hangover from hell...well...it's too much,' he said pulling the covers up around his chest and closing his eyes. 'I'm really sorry for what I said the other night. It must be really hard for you.'

'No. It's fine.'

Mack opened his eyes. 'Liar. I can see it in your face,' he smiled at her.

'You can make it up to me.'

'Yeah, how?'

'Speak to your father. He might be able to help.'

Mack snorted. 'Yeah right! He can't even bare to look at me, let alone speak to me.'

'If you speak first he'll be fine. I'd suggest you get up and have a shower first though. Make yourself look a little respectable at least.' She got up from the bed and headed to the door.

'OK.'

'Oh, and refrain from swearing,' she smiled as she closed the door.

***

His father was sitting at the long wooden table in the kitchen, reading the morning paper. The sunlight shone through the patio doors and normally, Mack would have appreciated the beauty of the day, but he wasn't in the mood. Partly due to the hangover, partly the impending conversation with his father.

He pulled out a chair and sat down opposite his father. He didn't look up. There was a pot of fresh coffee on the table and Mack helped himself to a much needed mug. He took a sip and cleared his throat, 'Dad', he paused, 'can I talk to you?'

His father continued reading for a moment longer before slowly folding up the paper and laying it down in front of him. He poured a coffee. 'Do I have a choice?'

'Well, technically, yeah you do, but I was kind of hoping you'd agree. I…this isn't easy for me, but I wanted to say I'm sorry.'

'For?'

'Well, firstly, for saying what I did the other night. I shouldn't have dragged it up, especially in front of mum. But mainly for letting you all down and for cheating on Jen. I know I've been a complete idiot and ruined everything. You don't need to tell me that, but I understand you're angry and need to vent your anger.' He sighed, 'To be honest, I don't think you can be any angrier than me.'

'Well, I understand that much at least. God knows I was angry at myself all those years ago.'

'Apparently, I can no longer take the moral high ground. It's ironic isn't it? All these years I've held it against you and I go and do exactly the same thing. For no real reason, that's what pisses me off the most. I mean, it's not as though Jen and I weren't getting on or were arguing all the time. There was actually nothing wrong with our relationship, far from it. At least you had some sort of reason,'

His father looked up quickly, 'Oh?'

Mack hesitated, 'Well, I mean I'm assuming there was some reason…' he tailed off.

His father nodded, 'well, reason is a bit strong, because really there can never be a good reason. I don't know, it was so long ago, it's kind of faded into the dim and distant past, which is how I wanted it. But if I'm honest, there wasn't really anything I could put my finger on. It wasn't as though your mother and I were unhappy, I think it was just that our circumstances had changed and I didn't cope with that very well. Nothing I can say will make it right, but work was stressful and I felt a great burden to work as hard as I could to make sure I could give you all the best, and I suppose I felt under pressure and I couldn't share that with your mother. I didn't want to burden her with my worries as she had enough to cope with. I'd come home every night and could see the strain she was under. I could hardly pour out all my stresses. She seemed increasingly distracted and uninterested. After a hard day at work, what I really wanted to do was come home and unwind, but the moment I walked in your mother expected me to take over the reins or at least help out, and if I'm honest, I began to resent it sometimes. Now though, looking back, I realise she'd had a hard day as well, it was just different, and if I didn't help out, then her hard day continued. It was a difficult time, there's no doubt about that, but…well,' he sighed, speaking to himself rather than Mack, 'I don't know, I didn't go looking for someone else, but it was as if she just appeared at the right time.'

'At first I was flattered at the interest she showed in me. She would listen to my worries, my stresses, laugh at my jokes… pathetic, I know,' he gave a tight lipped smile. 'I suspected she liked me, and I had no intention of it going any further, but I don't know, it just happened one evening

70

after work, and it was as if, once it happened, it was impossible to go back. I just got swept away with the whole thing. Every day I resolved to put an end to it, but I just found it so difficult. I was just weak I guess. Wanted my cake and all that. Does that make any sense?'

Mack nodded vigorously, 'Yes, yes it does. More than you can know. I know exactly what you mean. It's uncanny, it was kind of like it was for me. I can't possibly justify what I did, but I kind of felt powerless to stop it. I've had a lot of time to think things through and I know it was nothing to do with Jen and I, it was more like I just ended up developing feelings for someone else and as much as I knew it was wrong, and I didn't want it to happen, I just couldn't put a stop to it. I feel pathetic and weak and stupid. I am pathetic and weak and stupid.'

His father shook his head, 'You're human. You make mistakes like the rest of us. The question is, are you man enough to deal with them? You can sit upstairs and wither away, or you can face it head on. Admit you've made a huge mistake and pay the consequences. My one piece of advice is, don't let it ruin you. If Jen won't take you back, you need to accept and rebuild your life without her. It'll be hard, but you don't have a choice.'

'Easy for you to say. Mum took you back at least,' he said, not in a bitter way, just matter of factly.

'I know and I thank my lucky stars every day for it. I was a fool. I came this close to losing all of you,' he said, using his forefinger and thumb to indicate a small gap. They sat in silence for a few moments, each absorbed in their own thoughts.

'Can I ask you something?' his father asked.

'Do I have a choice?' he laughed.

'No!' he smiled. 'You were the youngest, what, two when it all happened? And yet you've held it against me the most. Why is that? Do you actually remember it?'

'No, not really, but I lived with the threat of it all happening again. Whenever you had a fall out or an argument, Kirsten would get worried that you were going to split up and John would have to console her and whenever I asked about it they clammed up and told me not to worry, so I ended up doing just that! Worrying you were going to leave. So, I don't know, maybe I began to resent you for it. Something like that. I've never given it a lot of thought to be honest, I just knew I was pissed off at you.'

'Thanks,' his father said solemnly.

'Can I ask you something?'

'Go ahead.'

'Well, I don't quite know how to put this, it's a bit delicate.' He saw his father's face redden. 'Oh no, nothing like that, nothing embarrassing.'

'Glad to hear it.' He said, visibly relieved. 'Ask away then.'

'Well, it's just that, I'll be devastated if Jen won't give it another go, I really will, but… I still can't shake the feelings I have for Abbi. I really liked her… loved her. I didn't expect that to happen and it just kind of took me by surprise when it did, and it's… I don't know, it's hard just to stop loving someone all of a sudden' he said abashed, not used to saying these things in front of his father, 'I… well, to put it bluntly, I've really fucked up on both counts. I've lost two women I cared for really deeply. Does that make any sense to you?'

He thought he saw a glint of anger flash across his father's face. He wasn't sure if it was his language or his admission. He quickly smoothed it over, adding, 'It's just that, you're the only person who might possibly understand. I could never admit that to anyone else.'

His father nodded, relaxing, seeming to understand. 'I do see you what you mean, although that in no way admonishes what you've done, but yes, I think if you developed feelings for the girl, you've left yourself in a bit of a pickle. Who was she?'

'Who, Abbi?'

'Is that her name?' his father asked curtly. He clearly wasn't comfortable talking about her. He probably felt he was being disloyal to Jen.

'Yeah, Abbi. Who was she? Whew,' Mack puffed his cheeks and exhaled slowly. 'She was just someone I met at a party. Well, I actually met her a few years ago at a bus stop, and we got chatting, but that was as far as it went. I didn't see her again after that, until, by chance I bumped into her at a party one night about a year ago.' He thought back to that night.

***

It amazed him how a simple twist of fate could alter things so drastically. Jen should have been with him that night, but she had decided at the last minute to go for a girl's weekend with her best friend and two other girls from work. It was a spur of the moment thing. They'd found a good deal and booked it a few days beforehand. Mack had no great objection and had gone ahead with his plans to meet some friends for a few drinks. They were in boisterous spirits after the pubs closed and no one was in the mood to call it a night, so they headed to a party of a friend of a friend, and that was it.

He made up his mind in the first few minutes that it was a pretty boring party and he planned to leave after finishing his drink and that's when he spotted her. She was standing in the hall, looking bored, and slightly disappointed, as if she really didn't want to be there but it was better than sitting at home watching The Jonathon Ross Show. He had this image of her leaving the party and walking home alone, feeling downhearted that another uneventful weekend had passed, and another humdrum week ahead loomed. He instinctively wanted to save her from that. He wanted her to go into work on Monday feeling happy and excited, so he headed over before she went off in search of her coat.

He didn't intentionally go out to have an affair. It wasn't even as if his sole purpose that evening was to get her into bed but he felt something for her the moment he met her. Right away, he was struck by how different she was from Jen. Jen was lively and vivacious, always the centre of attention. People were drawn to her, knowing they'd have a great time if she was there. Nights out were often organised around Jen's availability. The most appealing thing about Jen though, was that she wasn't fully aware that she had that effect on people. She wasn't the type to manipulate people so she could remain the centre of attention. It just happened naturally. She was a warm, fun, caring person, genuinely interested in people, and that's why everyone loved her. Not that Abbi wasn't warm and caring, it's just that she came across differently. She was quieter, more introvert, but not, as Mack had first assumed, lacking in confidence. She actually was very confident and assertive, but she didn't have a pressing need to talk all the time, fill the gaps in a conversation or to get her point of view across. She was happy to sit back and listen and offer an opinion or a comment if the situation allowed.

She was pretty as well, although again, in a different way. Jen was striking in her appeal. You could see her beauty at a distance. Abbi's beauty was less obvious initially however on closer inspection each individual feature was beautiful.

Her hair was styled into a sleek shiny bob and framed her dainty, angular face. She had large brown eyes with a slightly sad, almost melancholy look, but it added a softness to her features. But most of all it was her mouth. She had the softest, fullest, most kissable lips he'd encountered.... apart from Jen. He found himself staring at her mouth as she talked and laughed. He could see her lips moving but had no idea what she was saying. He was mesmerised by their pale pink hue.

He had honestly tried his hardest to refrain from getting involved with her, but the only way he could describe it was that it felt as if he was being sucked into a slow moving whirlpool, invisible forces pulling him in, engulfing him until he was powerless to escape their clutches.

He was drawn from that night when they left the party and walked to the pub. She was easy company and he knew she was attracted to him. He could have stopped it then, but he didn't. He wanted to be the man she thought he was. He could see she was happy, excited almost. Her eyes sparkled as she spoke and lit up when she laughed. She had a beautiful smile and Mack was acutely aware of the effect he was having on her. He could literally see her coming alive and he desperately wanted to be the person she was falling for. Even in those first few hours, he realised he couldn't let her down. He couldn't bear to see the disappointment on her face when he told her he was in love with someone else, so, rightly or wrongly, he said nothing. At the time, he stupidly convinced himself he was doing it with good intention, however, he realised that awful Sunday, that there was never anything good that was going to come of it. Perhaps, subconsciously, he had hoped she would get tired of him and be the one to break it off. That would have been the easy way out.

In the end, he'd hurt the two people he cared about deeply, and got her involved in something against her knowledge. Would it have been different had she known the truth? Who knew? She was adamant that she wouldn't have become involved and he no reason to disbelieve her. He knew he was being deceitful on many levels and it was this part of him that surprised him the most. He had no idea he could be like that and it wasn't something he was proud of.

***

'What was she like?' Mack's father broke into his thoughts.

Mack felt a bit uncomfortable talking out loud about her, it was if he was betraying Jen somehow and he knew his father really wouldn't feel comfortable speaking about her. He hesitated. 'She was nice, I mean really nice actually. It wasn't... none of this was her fault. She didn't know. I mean, not to begin with,' he said sheepishly.

'Right, I see.'

'Do you? I wish I did.'

'No, I don't see. It's just an expression.'

His father walked over and patted him on the shoulder. 'I've always said that there's something good to come out of even the very worst of situations. If things don't work out for you, it'll be a harsh lesson, but you'll survive it. You might not be the same person once you're over the worst if it, but the best you can do is to learn from it and don't make the same mistakes again.'

Mack shook his head. 'I've made such a mess of things, I can't see that anything good can come of it. I'm such an arse hole.'

'Yep, but you're still my son, and no matter what you do I'll always be here for you. I let you down when you were young, but it has always been my intention to be here for you ever since.'

It dawned on Mack that as much as there were similarities between his own behaviour and his father's, there was also one fundamental difference, which ironically meant his father was the better man, in his eyes anyway. His father, on realising his mother knew, actively ended the relationship and committed to his mother. He made a decision, something that Mack hadn't been able to do at any point. In fact, he'd actively buried his head in the sand, which had cost him two women.

'Look, if I can give you a piece of advice. Think about what you want, *who* you want, and make your case, plead and beg if necessary. At least try to fight for what you want. If it doesn't pay off, then what have you lost? Nothing! If you don't fight for what you want then you may live to regret it, and that will be the biggest mistake you'll make. You're a fighter Mack. I've seen it since you were this high,' he said raising his hand a short distance from the ground, 'I've seen your grit and determination, that competitive streak which makes you dig in and give it one hundred percent. Let's see some of that now eh?'

Mack nodded, feeling tearful but suddenly energized. 'You always knew how to give a good pep talk dad'. The thought of it scared him, like nothing ever had before, but he knew he had no choice. He had to give himself a fighting chance at least.

It took him the best part of an hour to think what he wanted to say, but he felt a sense of relief and achievement as he sealed the envelopes and wrote the addresses on the front. He had two letters; one explaining how sorry he was and asking for forgiveness, the other, explaining how sorry he was, asking for forgiveness and a second chance. He'd decided to write letters because he knew neither of them would take his call or agree to meet him. The most he could hope for was that they'd read a letter. He put stamps on the envelopes and headed out to post them immediately, before he had a chance to change his mind.

His mood was considerably lighter when he returned home. He knew it was out of his hands now, at least for a short while. If there was no response or the answer was *no* to his plea for a second chance, then he needed to think about what he would do next and how much he should pursue it. One step at a time, he told himself.

He rewarded himself with a cold beer and an evening of marking algebra homework. He finished with a bath, a shave and an early night. He felt refreshed in the morning and more like himself than he had done in days. Of course, he knew it could all come crashing down around him depending on the response to his letter, assuming there was one of course.

Chapter 4
Abbi

Abbi took another sip of coffee and cleared her throat before beginning. She was apprehensive about revealing too much to Jen. She kept things close to her chest at the best of times and here she was, about to disclose personal information to a complete stranger.

She tried to remember when it began to dawn on her that all wasn't well with her relationship with Mack, but in all honesty she didn't ever recall being outrightly suspicious. She just knew things were a little different from her previous relationship, not that she could really use that as a gold standard. Looking back, there were lots of small things, which individually didn't mean much, but in hindsight should have set alarm bells ringing.

He had a vagueness when it came to conversations about what he did on the nights they weren't together and about previous relationships. She put the latter down to just being a man and having a reluctance to talk about anything which remotely involved emotions. As to his whereabouts, she knew he had a wide circle of friends and did lots of different activities, so she didn't question it too much. Some nights he stayed, some nights he didn't. That's just the way it had always been. It didn't bother her too much as she was always busy with her thesis.

What she did notice was the lack of sex in the beginning. They would often meet up back at her flat and spend the evening talking, drinking wine and getting acquainted on the sofa, but it never got past the kissing stage. She tried occasionally to move it on, but he always gently resisted. At first, she put it down to a desire to take things slowly, but if so, he was different to every other man she'd known, not that she'd known many.

Eventually, she took matters into her own hands. He had arranged to come round after football training on Friday night as usual. She had prepared a meal, set the table and lit some candles, making it look romantic but not too obvious.

She had a soak in the bath with some aromatic oils and took extra care in getting ready. She decided on tight jeans with a fitted shirt revealing just a small amount of cleavage. Her hair was easy, falling naturally into a bob, but she applied a light amount of makeup, finishing it off with some pale pink lip gloss.

It seemed to have the desired effect on Mack, although he did appear a little edgy when he saw the table, candles and low lighting. 'Woah, what's all this?' he asked nervously.

'Oh, nothing really, I just thought it would be nice to have a relaxed meal, I don't really get the chance to cook very often. I hope you like lasagne,' she said, pouring him a glass of red wine. She reached up to kiss him but she noticed that he cut it short.

'Sounds great. I'm starving,' he disentangled himself from her and bent down to look in the oven. I hope it's not too long to wait.'

'No, it should be ready now actually. Have a seat and I'll dish up,' she smiled.

'I didn't have you down as the domestic kind.'

'No? Why's that then? Is it because I've got a degree in physics? Do you think that means I can't do anything remotely girly?'

'No, no, not that, I just meant…' he stammered, smiling sheepishly, 'sorry, I don't really know what I meant.' He reached over for her hand and rubbed it gently. 'You've gone to a lot of effort,' he said, changing the subject, 'thanks, I appreciate it.'

'Not really, it didn't take that long and I …I enjoyed doing it, getting things ready for you coming round,' she smiled bashfully. She knew she sounded like a 1950s housewife, but there was something comforting and pleasing about the thought of preparing dinner for him coming home. She was wary about what she said though. She didn't want to scare him off.

He laughed awkwardly and took a large drink of wine. She changed the subject quickly, trying not to ruin the atmosphere. 'Speaking of non-girly things, did I tell you I wasted half of the morning changing my tyre?'

'No,' he shook his head, 'how come? And how do you know how to change a tyre? I'm not being sexist. There are some blokes who wouldn't know what to do?'

'Well, I had a flat tyre, must have been a slow puncture and I did a mechanics course when I bought my first car. My dad insisted.'

'Are there no ends to your talents?'

'Nope, and there's still many you haven't seen,' she said, raising her eyebrows. She thought she saw a flicker of something in his eyes, but she didn't know what. It was so subtle, she dismissed it. She kept the conversation light and

81

she could see him begin to relax as the evening wore on. A few more glasses of wine and he was back to his usual self, laughing and joking. Once they'd finished their meal, they moved over to the sofa and curled up together as they usually did. Abbi felt the effects of the alcohol wash over her, diminishing her inhibitions. She moved her body closer to his and placing her hand on his jaw, turned his face towards her. She could see the rise and fall of his chest under his shirt, slow and steady, and the thought of his naked flesh next to hers, urged her on. She moved her hand to the back of his head, pulling his face down towards her. She reached up and kissed him, slowly at first, trying to convey her feelings. Mack responded, pulling her head towards his. She ran her hands up over his shirt and felt him tense. She could tell he was about to resist her, as he had done these past few weeks, but she didn't give him the chance. She slipped her hand inside and moved it up over his taught stomach. She felt him flinch as she did so, taking a sharp intake of breath, but she took this to mean he was enjoying it. Her kisses became more intense, her tongue reaching inside his mouth, searching for his. He pulled back, 'Abbi...' he sounded hoarse, 'I... eh...'

'Shhh,' she said, placing her fingers over his lips. She twisted her body round and straddled him, slowly undoing the buttons on her shirt. He was about to protest again but stopped when she slipped her shirt off, shedding it to the floor. He stared at her momentarily but before he could protest any further, she closed her lips around his again and taking his hands placed them on her bare skin. She could feel the heat of his hands burn into her flesh and she longed to feel them explore her body further. She pulled back from him and he sat, unmoving, hands still on her waist. She quickly undid her bra and let it drop to the floor. She could feel him respond beneath her. His hands moved slowly, over her waist and round towards her breasts. He stopped momentarily, but as she bent forward to kiss him again she felt his hands cup them, rolling her nipples slowly between his thumbs and forefingers. She moaned into his mouth, pushing herself into him, urging him on. Their movements quickened. She removed his shirt and felt his flesh against hers. She wanted more. She needed to feel him inside her and sat up quickly, taking him by surprise.

'What?' he asked.

She unbuckled his belt and the buttons on his jeans and moved her hand inside. She watched him intently as he closed his eyes and laid his head back against the sofa. She took him in her hands, feeling him push into her. She bent her head, kissing his neck and chest as she continued to work her hands. Mack gasped and groaned as she moved her mouth down, removing his jeans as she did so.

'Oh God Abbi,' he said gruffly, 'If you keep doing that I'll......'

She looked up and smiled, 'sorry, I wouldn't want to rush things,' she said, slowly removing her own jeans and underwear. She caught a flash of something on his face, a moment's hesitation, was he about to try and stop things going any further? She didn't want to lose the moment. She closed her hands around him and moved them slowly, squeezing him gently. Mack closed his eyes again. She moved her position to straddle him, guiding him inside her. She closed her own eyes and arched her body, feeling the fullness of him inside her. She moved slowly at first, enjoying the feeling of him pushing into her. She wanted the moment to last forever. Mack's more or less passive involvement so far suddenly changed. She felt his movements quicken and he grasped her hips, pulling her down hard onto him as he did his best to push himself up. She moved in time with him, clasping his hands at her hips. She felt him tense and push one last time, finally relaxing, letting out a deep moan as he did so.

Abbi bent down to kiss him and he laughed, 'I believe you've just seduced me,' returning her kiss.

'I may have,' she said, still moving herself slowly on top of him. She wasn't usually this forward when it came to sex, but it occurred to her that Mack didn't know this. She enjoyed the feeling of taking the lead, playing the seductress. 'Shall we move somewhere more comfortable?' she asked, nodding in the direction of the bedroom.

They headed through to her room taking the wine with them. They climbed under the covers and Abbi was clearly ready for more but Mack just laughed and pulled her in close to him, her head resting on his chest. 'Come here,' he said gently, 'I need some recovery time. I wasn't expecting that.'

They must have both dozed off for a while. Abbi had no idea how long for or what time it was when she woke, feeling him behind her. He moved closer to her and she felt his hands stroke her thighs. He ran his fingers up the outside of her thigh, making her shiver, then let them slowly drift over her hip bone, across her stomach and down, working his fingers expertly around the soft flesh at the top of her thighs. She gasped as she felt his fingers moving inside her, probing deeply. She turned to face him, reaching for his face, bringing it down to meet her lips. Mack rolled her onto her back and she wrapped her legs around his hips, locking him into position. She moaned loudly as she felt him push himself into her. Her hips rose up to meet him as he pushed deeper. She reached her hands around him and sunk her nails into the flesh of his buttocks, trying to push him as deep as she could. They moved together, slowly to begin with, enjoying the sensation of their bodies rubbing together, their flesh moist with sweat as their pace increased. She could feel the sensation rise deep within her and she tried to hold onto it, making it last but she couldn't hold back any longer, crying out with every thrust he made, the sensation rising deep in her pelvis. Weeks of pent up frustration poured out of her as he pushed into her one last time. The feeling spread out over her stomach and thighs. She was gasping and moaning at the same time. The sensation continuing, her body contracting and relaxing until she let out a deep breath and collapsed back onto the bed.

'Oh my God, 'she said, genuinely surprised, 'that's… I've never…' she stopped, not sure what to say.

Mack looked down and laughed gently, 'has that never happened before?'

'Well, no, not like that. I mean I've had an orgasm, at least I think I have, but not quite like that. 'My legs…,' she said in astonishment.

'Turned to jelly?'

'Yeah. Obviously that's not new to you then?'

'Eh, no,' he said sheepishly, 'I've eh, known it to happen before.'

'Wow, I hope it happens all the time.'

'Right, no pressure on me then!'

She laughed and reached up to kiss him. 'I'm sure you can manage that again. You seem to know what you're doing.'

He laughed, 'maybe.'

'How many girlfriends have you had then?' she asked innocently. She definitely saw it then. A shadow passed over him. The jokiness lost. 'I eh, I don't really go in for all that past history stuff and to be honest, it's not how many girlfriends I've had or how often I've had sex. Good sex is about the person you're with. It can be really crap if it's with the wrong person, do you know what I mean?'

'Yeah, I guess, although I haven't had sex with many different people so I don't have a lot to compare it to. What I do know though, is that so far, that's been the best.'

'Ha, glad to hear you enjoyed it. Come on,' he said tucking her head into the nook of his arm, 'it's the middle of the night, let's get some sleep.' He kissed the top of her head, signaling the end of their conversation.

***

Things ticked along smoothly for the next few months after that. When she wasn't studying she worked part time giving extra physics tuition to school pupils which left very little free time. People asked her afterwards how come she didn't suspect anything but it didn't really seem that unusual to her at the time. It wasn't until she'd finished the PhD and had more free time to think about a life outside work that she began to have doubts here and there, but even then, she didn't know if they would have turned into full scale suspicions if it hadn't have been for her friend, Julia.

They didn't meet up very often, but when they did meet, like all true friends, they picked up exactly where they had left off. Abbi was taking a much needed break one Saturday afternoon and had agreed to meet Julia for lunch. Julia was vivacious and outgoing, where Abbi was quieter and more reserved, but Julia had a way of gleaning information out of her. The moment they sat down, Julia noticed a difference in her, which could have been down to the fact that she had just come from sharing a bed with Mack an hour ago

'You look great!' Julia declared. 'Being stuck in a lab twenty four seven must suit you!'

'Ha,' she laughed, 'even I'm not that sad.'

'No?'

'No!' Abbi said, kicking her gently under the table.

'So what is it that's giving you that rosy glow? Have you discovered some potion for eternal youth?'

'I'm doing physics remember.'

'Oh yeah. Well something's agreeing with you.'

'Mmm,' she shrugged, taking a sip of her wine.

'Abbi, come on, your face is a dead giveaway. Have you found a man?'

She sighed, 'God, how do you do that? Nobody else has asked.'

'That's because you're surrounded by physicists. So, who is he? Anyone I know? And how come I haven't met him?'

'Ok, slow down, so many questions. His name is Mack and no you don't know him, and yes, he's great before you ask.'

'Wow! You've never described anyone as great before. Not even Steven, although admittedly, Steven should never be used as a gold standard boyfriend. He was an arsehole, but let's not go there.'

'I'm not. I didn't mention Steven, you did, and I'm not *going anywhere* because I can't get a word in edge ways!'

Abbi filled her in over the next few hours and Julia seemed impressed and pleased for her, until she asked some crunch questions, such as where did he live What were his friends like and did she have any photos of him. Abbi was a bit sketchy on some of the detail here and Julia was quick to pick up on it.

'Wait a moment, run this by me again. You've been seeing him for what? Almost five months? And you've never been to his flat or met his friends or family? Doesn't that seem odd?'

'Well, it didn't, but now you mention it, maybe a little. I haven't given it much thought because I've been so tied up with my thesis. Even if he had asked me out to meet his family or friends I probably wouldn't have the time.'

'Abbi! Don't make excuses. Look, I haven't met him and maybe I'm just being overly suspicious but some of these things don't really add up. You can find out easily-just ask if you can meet at his flat one night.'

'Mmm, I'll see. I'm not that bothered. You've been in one too many rubbish relationships. That's why you're so suspicious.'

'Yeah, maybe,' Julia laughed. 'It's really none of my business. I would like to meet him though.'

'Yeah, I'd like that too.' Abbi mused, but she wasn't sure of Julia's motives.

***

She had enjoyed lunch with Julia, but felt a bit deflated as she walked home. She tried to recall events over the last few months. Was there room for suspicion she wondered? It was true, she didn't know much about him. She hadn't met his friends or family and Julia had pointed out that, in her opinion, you didn't really know someone properly until you'd seen them in their home surroundings. She'd brought up the subject of his friends before but he brushed it off, saying they were a bunch of hooligans and reprobates and she really wasn't missing anything by not meeting them. As for his flat, the explanation had been simple enough. He shared it with a couple of mates and he described it as a modern day *Men Behaving* badly scenario. A bit like his friends, he didn't think there was much to be gained by meeting his flat mates or seeing his flat. He said he would need a week off work to clean it up before letting her step foot over the door. Her flat, he pointed out was cleaner and more hospitable than his own, and they generally would have more time alone together in her flat. She had accepted this without question. Why wouldn't she?

With Steven, it had been obvious from the start that he was playing around with other women. He flirted with everyone he met and didn't really make any secret of the fact that he enjoyed the company of women. He also stated from the outset that he didn't believe in monogamous relationships and was way too young to settle down with one woman. She always knew when he had someone else on the go because he was cagey and vague about his plans. Mack had never been like that. Surely if was seeing someone else she'd have noticed something.

Well, she thought to herself, *it's easy enough to find out, I'll just ask him if we can go to his flat for a change or meet his friends for a drink.* Her mood brightened as she reached her flat, convincing herself that this really wasn't a problem. She felt her face flush with embarrassment. What would Mack think of her? What would he say if he knew the questions which were going through her head? He'd think she was an idiot and would probably be either disappointed or mad that she could think such a thing.

It was a few days before she heard from him. This was normal for them, however, given her underlying uneasiness, it had felt like a long wait. She checked her phone three or four times a day to see if he'd sent a message or an email. In fact, thinking about it, they mostly communicated via email, his work email. Was that odd? Probably. Most people used plain old text or an app of some sort. And why a work email?

He emailed her on Thursday to organise Friday, which was their usual night for seeing each other, usually after his football training. She even began to suspect that. Did he really go to training? He normally turned up with his kit bag and obviously she'd never checked it to see if there was a sweaty football strip inside. She was pretty sure this wasn't a lie as he lived and breathed football and often gave her a full synopsis of the training or the match over a glass of wine, oblivious to the fact that she wasn't really that interested.

He arrived on Friday night as usual and dumped his kit bag in the hall. He kissed her and handed her a bottle of wine as he made his way into the kitchen. 'Something smells good,' he said, heading to the cooker to check what was cooking. He picked up the lid of one of the pots and peered in. 'Mmm, curry, my favourite. Smells great.'

'Good, hopefully it'll taste as good as it smells,' she said, handing him a glass of wine.

'Oh, thanks, I need this after the day I've had.' He stopped for a moment, looking her up and down, 'You look particularly sexy tonight, planning something special?' he asked, pulling her towards him. She could taste the red wine as he kissed her fully on the lips.

'How long did you say dinner would be?'

'I didn't, but it'll be about five minutes.'

'Shame,' he said nuzzling her neck, 'I'm hungry for something else entirely.'

She gently prised him away. 'You'll just have to control yourself and be patient then won't you? And who knows, if you're good and behave yourself you might just be rewarded with a tasty dessert.'

She noticed he smelt fresh, as if he'd had a shower. This was always the case, but now she wondered if that was because he'd been with someone else rather than at training. She resisted the temptation to look inside his bag. She shook herself. *Don't be ridiculous.*

She returned to the cooker and concentrated on stirring the curry. She wanted to say something now, perhaps just a casual mention of meeting his friends, but her heart was in her mouth. She could feel the pulse in her neck, hammering against her skin so hard she was sure he could see it. *No! Not yet. I'll wait until we've eaten and are relaxing. I don't want to spoil things this early on.*

Mack was in a chirpy mood and didn't pick up on any reservations in Abbi's mood. She felt herself watching and listening to him more intently. She noticed that most of his conversation was about his work, football and other hobbies. He was about to start training for a marathon so he was talking about a training plan and trying to decide on whether to give up alcohol. It was all fairly neutral she noticed. No depth. No mention of family and not much about friends.

She interrupted him abruptly, asking, 'so where do you get all this sportiness from? Is your brother as sporty as you?'

'Eh, yeah, a bit I guess, nowhere near as good as me though,' he joked.

'Obviously.' She poured him another glass of wine, 'here, you better make the most of this before you start serious training. 'So, who do you take after then? Your dad? Did he do many sports?'

'Mmm, he did a few sports in his younger years. You're full of questions tonight. Why all the sudden interest?'

'Mmm? Oh no real reason, just curious that's all,' she replied, trying to keep her tone casual, almost disinterested. 'You don't speak about your family that much. I'd like to meet them. See if you're anything like them. Hear stories about you when you were young, that sort of thing.'

He stared at her, open mouthed. She wasn't imagining it, he did look shocked and deeply uncomfortable. 'Right. Well, that's fine, but I don't really go in for all that sort of thing.'

'What sort of thing?'

'Well, you know, meeting the parents and all that. It's all a bit kind of formal and false.'

'Yeah, but surely you have to meet someone's family at some point. I mean, are they not curious about me?'

'No, they're not really that fussed about snooping around in my personal affairs.'

'It's hardly snooping around. It's just asking a pretty normal question I would have thought. My mum and dad are keen to meet you, for what it's worth.'

'What? You've told them about me? What the..? When did you tell them about me?'

'Calm down. What's the big deal? I told them about you ages ago. My mum always asks if I'm seeing anyone, so why would I lie?'

'No, I'm not suggesting you should lie, I just…I don't know, I'm just surprised that you didn't mention it to me that's all. I'm just not all that comfortable with the whole *meet the parents* thing'

'I know, so you said!' she replied more sharply than she intended, 'don't worry, I won't invite you for Sunday lunch any time soon.'

He smiled weakly and drained his wine. 'Shall we open another bottle?'

'I thought we might go out for a change? What about The Bailey? That must be your local is it not.'

She watched him carefully. He swallowed hard and ran his fingers through his hair. 'What?' he asked moodily, 'you want to go all the way across town? I don't mind going out but why don't we just go down the road?'

'Because we always go the pub down the road. I just thought it would be a nice change to go somewhere different, somewhere in your end of town.'

'God, what's with you tonight?' he said jumping up from the sofa, 'all of a sudden you're unhappy that we always do the same thing. You've never mentioned it before. Why now? Why all of a sudden? Are you unhappy with the way things are?'

'No,' she said slowly, 'but there's nothing wrong with wanting to do something different is there? It's fine, don't worry about it, we can go some other time.'

'No, we can head out for a quick drink if you like, I just can't be bothered traipsing all the way across town, to have to head back over here again.'

She could have pointed out the obvious, that they could have stayed at his, but she decided not to push it for the time being. She flicked through the channels and settled for Doc Martin, as if to prove a point. She wasn't quite sure what the point was, but she felt a sense of self-righteousness. She put the remote control on the table and headed through to the kitchen to get another bottle of wine.

They passed the rest of the evening in a subdued silence watching random programmes, but neither really concentrating. Abbi mulled over their conversation, picking it to pieces, analysing every comment and every shift in body language. The more she went over it, the more flustered and irritated she became, until she could no longer bare to sit next to him

'I'm off to bed,' she bristled. They hadn't ever argued before and they hadn't exactly argued now, but there was a definite frostiness between them. He nodded, still staring at the TV, and she didn't kiss him, as she might have done normally.

She delayed as much as possible, brushing her teeth, taking longer to remove her make-up and get ready for bed than usual, hoping he'd join her, and they could smooth things over, but there was no sign of him.

She climbed into bed with mixed feelings. Part of her felt angry and upset, part of her felt stupid. Had she started an argument over nothing? She couldn't tell but she did feel his behaviour and response had been unreasonable. The problem was that she didn't feel she could speak to anyone or get an unbiased opinion. Julia had already formed her own opinion and this would just confirm it. She heard the click of the TV as he turned it off and she lay, tense, almost holding her breath, waiting for him to come to bed. She must have drifted off to sleep at some point, but it was a restless sleep and she didn't at any point hear him coming to bed.

When she woke in the morning, there was no sign of him. His side of the bed hadn't been slept in. It was eight 'o' clock. The flat was silent. She got up slowly and went through to the living room, half expecting to find him asleep on the sofa, but he wasn't there either. There was a note on the table.

Have got quite a bit of work to do today so I headed off early this morning. Will call you during the week. Mack

That was it! Not even a kiss at the end of the letter. He was well and truly pissed off with her, but if he had nothing to hide, why would he have reacted in that way? She couldn't concentrate for the rest of the day, continually turning it over in her head. Every so often she'd pick up the note and read it again, each time, becoming more and more despondent, until eventually she threw it in the bin. She couldn't bare to look at it anymore. As much as she didn't want to tell Julia, she needed someone to talk to.

***

'He said what? That's weird. You weren't exactly asking probing questions, I mean you just asked a fairly straightforward, normal question about his family, who, personally speaking, I think you should have met by now. And the fact that he hasn't even mentioned you to them, that's really strange. I think you're going to have to confront him.'

'But what if I confront him and it's not true? How stupid will I look? And also, will he ever trust me again?'

'Him trust you! It's the other way round. You have to earn someone's trust, and right now I'd say he's done nothing to earn it. Exactly the opposite in fact, he's really testing your trust right now.'

'Yeah, I guess so,' she sighed. 'I don't know, I wouldn't even know where to start.'

'No,' Julia said slowly, 'It's difficult,' she said absent mindedly, 'Hmm,' she sighed, 'I can't really think of any other reason he would be acting so strangely, unless… you don't think he's…'

'Oh don't say he's gay, for God's sake Julia,' she laughed humorlessly.

'No! I was going to say, do you think he might be… religious or something?'

'What!' Abbi burst out laughing properly this time, 'Oh Julia, you make it sound like something clandestine.'

'No, I didn't mean it like that, but it might make sense if you think about it. Maybe he's quite religious but he's not sure how to tell you, because you're a physicist and a non-believer. Maybe he thinks you'll laugh at him or worse, dump him.'

'Julia! For one thing, I know I don't believe in God but that's nothing to do with me studying physics. The two things aren't mutually exclusive, in fact many scientists believe that science and nature are proof that God exists, but that's another matter. Anyway, I still fail to see how you've arrived at this conclusion.'

'Well, it might explain why he never stays on a Saturday, because he's always got to go to church on a Sunday.'

'And how does it explain him not introducing me to his family or friends, not staying over at his flat?'

'Maybe they're all religious too. Maybe his family wouldn't approve of you sleeping together. Maybe his friends wouldn't either.'

'Right! First you have him labeled as a philanderer and now as belonging to some strange religious cult. Honestly,' she rolled her eyes, 'I've heard it all now.'

'Yeah, sorry, I was getting carried away. It is a bit farfetched. I'll stick to the two-timer theory. So, what are you going to do?' she asked, signaling to the waiter for more drinks.

'Do you think he's just a commitment freak?'

'No, I still think his reaction was strange.'

'Hmm, well then, unfortunately I think I'm going to have to ask him. I mean I could fish a bit more first. I could suggest meeting him at his flat or in Stockbridge, but I have a feeling he'll just make an excuse of some sort. I'll need to re-establish contact first.'

'Have you heard from him since Friday?'

'No,' Abbi replied miserably. 'I started emailing him a few times but stopped. I was hoping he'd get in touch with me first. I kind of feel the onus is on him.'

'I agree, it is, but you might have to bite the bullet and swallow your pride if you want to find out the truth.'

'I'm not sure what to say, but I might as well make a start.' She fished her phone out of her pocket and started tapping After a few moments she said 'Right. This is what I've typed so far. *Hi Mack, sorry about Friday…*'

Julia held her hand up, stopping Abbi before she could go any further. 'No wait, don't start by apologising. That's like saying it's all your fault. Why not just say something like, *Mack, I'm not sure what happened on Saturday night,* but…' she thought for a moment, '*but I obviously touched a nerve. I didn't mean to upset you, but whatever happened, I don't think it's worth us falling out about it.* I don't know, something like that. You're not apologising and you're being quite grown up about it. Just ask him to call you and then it's up to him.'

'Yeah, that sounds good,' she said tapping at her phone, 'I'll mail him just now.'

'No, text him instead. You said he tends to use emails more often. This might test him a bit.'

Abbi reluctantly agreed and sent a text before she could change her mind. Julia pushed a second glass of wine towards her and gave her a sympathetic smile. 'Look, I'm sure it will be fine. I hope it'll be fine, and if it's not, you deserve to know.'

'Thanks. I hope you're right.' She took a sip of her wine. 'I'm pretty sure he's not cheating on me though.'

'Well, you know him better than me. I'm sure you're right. Just out of interest, what would you do if he is?'

'I have no idea. Tell him where to go I guess.'

***

She heard nothing for a few days but on Friday morning she received an email, not a text or a phone call, but an email, from his work account.

Hi, sorry, maybe overreacted a bit. Had a bit of a stressful day. Will I come round tonight?

Her heart leapt when she saw she had an email from him, but she had mixed emotions about the content. It wasn't really an apology. It was almost dismissive in its tone and then just back to business as usual. No acknowledgment that anything had happened between them. She didn't reply at once. She closed the email and left it for a while. She became so absorbed in writing up her thesis that it was almost five by the time she looked up from her laptop. Now it would look like she was ignoring him and being childish.

She quickly sent a text which said *yes, fine, see you later*. She presumed it would be after football training, so in effect, no extra effort on his part.

She didn't cook. She was so fed up by that point that she decided if he wasn't intent on making an effort, then why should she?

She had no idea what she was going to say to him, but her heart was beating fast when she answered the door.

'Hi,' he said brightly, handing her a bunch of flowers and swooping down to kiss her. 'Sorry,' he said looking sheepish.

'Thanks,' she said dryly, following him through the kitchen, 'I'll find a vase for them later.' She put them on the table and folded her arms across her chest, making it clear she was waiting for an explanation.

'So, are you still talking to me?' he asked.

'That depends upon what you've got to say. I'm still a bit puzzled by your reaction. Where did you sleep? On the sofa, or did you just go home?'

'I slept on the sofa for a while, then headed home first thing in the morning. A bit dumb, I know. I don't know what got into me.'

'No, neither do I.'

He sighed, 'look, are you going to hold it against me and keep me in the dog house all night? I've said I'm sorry.'

'And what more can I ask for, right?' she said, shaking her head and pouring herself a glass of wine. She could tell they were headed for an argument, and as much as she hated confrontation, she wasn't inclined to let it go. 'I'm not asking for much. How long have we been seeing each other? Almost six months, and I've never met any of your friends. God, things were bad with Steven, but I'd met most of his friends by this stage, even some of his girlfriends. What is it? Are you embarrassed about me or something?'

'What, no! It's nothing like that.'

99

'Oh but it is something? What is it then?'

'It's nothing,' he sighed. 'Look, don't take this the wrong way, but I think you're making more of it than there is. I'm a bit insulted that you're comparing me to your ex. I mean, did he introduce you to his family?'

'No, he didn't, but this isn't about him, it's about you. For what it's worth, he was such a commitment phobe, there was no way he'd let any of his girlfriends meet his parents.'

'So, it was Ok for him, but not for me.'

'You're changing the subject. I've just said, this isn't about him.'

'So what is it about then?' he said shifting uncomfortably in his chair, resigned to having a conversation he didn't really want to have.

She was thrown momentarily by his directness. 'It's about, it's about... tell me honestly Mack, are you having an affair?'

She was surprised by how shocked he looked. He was pale and speechless. She hadn't meant to come out with it as abruptly as she did, but having done so, she expected him to deny it immediately. She was equally shocked when he didn't reply immediately.

'No, Jen, No, what the hell are you talking about?'

She felt her knees buckle and grabbed the back of the chair to steady herself. 'What did you just call me?'

'What?'

'Jen. You said Jen!'

'No... I...'

'Mack, don't even try to lie about. Oh my God, it's true, isn't it? Who's Jen and how long has it been going on?' she asked coldly

He leaned forward in his chair, resting his elbows on his knees and put his head in his hands.

He sat in silence.

'Mack! I asked you how long you've been having an affair?'

'I've... I'm not having an affair. I mean, not in the way you think. Technically, I'm not really having an affair with someone else'

'What? Mack I have no idea what you're talking about. If you're not having an affair with someone else who are you having an affair?'

'You.... It's you I'm having the affair with.'

She sat dumfounded, unable to make sense of what he was saying. 'Sorry... what do... I mean... what are you saying?'

'I'm saying, it's you I'm having the affair with. I'm with someone else. I've been with someone else for... a while.'

'What?' she whispered, 'what do you mean? How long have you been with her?' her blood ran cold as she recalled the name. *Jen*. When she first met Mack almost four years ago, she remembered his friends ribbing him about going home to his girlfriend, *Jen!* That couldn't be right. *No*, she dismissed the thought. She couldn't be sure that was the name, especially in her current state of mind.

She looked at him for some clue. His head was still in his hands. 'Mack! Look at me. Tell me you weren't with her when I met you at the bus stop that night.'

He couldn't deny it,

'Oh my God,' she dropped onto the kitchen seat in front of her.

'Abbi, I... look... I'm sorry... I can explain.'

'Sorry!' she shrieked, 'SORRY.' She picked up the coffee cup in front of her and hurled it at him with a force that surprised even her. Mack saw it just in time and ducked, leaving it to smash into the wall behind him, dark brown coffee streaking the crisp white walls. 'Get out, get out,' she screamed.

For a moment she thought he was going to try and placate her, but he obviously thought better of it and left, closing the door quietly behind him.

She sat at the table staring at the kitchen wall in disbelief. She knew she should clean the wall otherwise it would be sure to stain, but she couldn't move. She had no idea how long she sat there, but it was pitch dark when she eventually looked out of the kitchen window and she realised she was icy cold. She put the kettle on, but she had no interest in either making nor drinking tea, so she did the only thing that she could think of , which was to go to bed. She didn't bother undressing. She just climbed in to bed and numbly pulled the blanket over her. Once safely in the cocoon of her room, the tears began to flow and once started, she thought they would never stop. She went over it again and again, trying to make some sense of it, but the fact of the matter was, quite simply, there was no sense in any of it.

She felt as if the man she had fallen in love with was a total stranger. Adultery was wrong in her eyes. No question about it, regardless of whether someone was actually married or not. She would never go on a date with someone who already had a girlfriend, never mind get so deeply involved that she'd fall in love with them. Apart from the pain and anguish she felt at losing the man she loved, the overwhelming feeling building inside her was one of anger and resentment that she'd become unwittingly involved in a relationship that she felt was morally wrong. She felt disgusted with herself and was suffering waves of nausea at the thought of herself as adulteress. She couldn't believe he had lied to her for so long. She kept asking why? *What had made him do it? Why had he chosen her to do it with? Had he had affairs with lots of women or was she the first?* She felt like a victim, like prey which he had stalked, captured and spat out, having taken what he needed.

Every time she thought about Mack, pictured his face, she just couldn't see him as the same man who had delivered such devastating news. She couldn't make the connection between the two. Perhaps she would in time, perhaps it was just too fresh and raw at the moment. She hoped so, because more than anything she wanted to see them both as the same person so she could focus all her energy on hating him rather than wondering why.

She slowly fell apart in the days and weeks that followed. Julia came to her rescue and helped her through. She still had her thesis to write up and it was this which was the eventual catalyst, pulling her out of her reverie. She put her anger to good use and rather than feeling sorry for herself, she used it to work for her. She was determined that she wasn't going to let Mack ruin her or everything she'd been working for.

'Good girl,' Julia commended her, 'It would be a travesty if you gave up now. It's the best thing you can do. Throw yourself into your work. It'll take your mind of it.'

She hadn't heard from Mack at all since he had left that night, and although she knew she should be glad, and that even if he did get in touch, there's no way she'd respond, there was still a small part of her which secretly hoped he might try. She missed him even though she hated him. She would never admit it to anyone, but she found herself continually checking her phone and emails for messages.

A message did arrive when she was least expecting it. She was deep in concentration, proof reading the chapter she had just completed, when she heard her phone ping. She left it and eventually forgot about it until she took a break and went to make herself a much needed coffee. She was tired and her eyes ached; a combination of poor sleep and staring at a computer screen every day for the last few weeks.

She absentmindedly picked up phone, flicking through it whilst she made the coffee, when she remembered it had beeped earlier on. She had a message in her email inbox. Her heart missed a beat when she saw it was from Mack. She stared at it, wondering whether to just leave it. She laid the phone on the table and concentrated on making the coffee. She sat down cupping her hands around the mug, blowing on the steam rising from the surface. She looked at the phone, not sure what she was expecting to happen.

For fuck's sake, just open it. What can it possibly say that can hurt you anymore than he already has? She said out loud.

She picked up the phone quickly and tapped the email icon. She scanned the content to get the gist of it, then re-read it slowly.

Abbi, I'm not sure if you'll read this, but I hope so. I know it'll be a difficult decision but I hope you decided to open it and are reading it now. There are no words to express how sorry I am or wrong I know I've been. I know you're probably asking why, and I honestly don't know, but I feel I at least owe it to you to try and explain. I'll understand if you don't want to see me, but if you can find it in your heart to see me, just for one night, please get in touch. Mack x

She closed the email and thought for a moment. What point was there in agreeing to see him. Julia would say she should tell him where to go. She probably should. She should probably ignore the email altogether. Delete it, but there was something nagging at her, something tugging at her heart strings, urging her to say yes, just to see what he had to say. It was just natural curiosity, she assured herself.

Whatever she decided, she wouldn't answer straight away. She wasn't sure whether to speak to Julia about it, however, she later decided that she needed to speak it through with someone and Julia was the best person she could think of.

'What?' she spat, 'he's asking to see you? He's got a real nerve. What a bastard!' She took a sip of her coffee and seemed to reflect for a moment. 'Sorry, it's not about me or what I think though. What do you think? '

'Phwww, I have no idea,' she sighed, shoulders sagging as she mulled it over. 'I know I should just ignore his email, and don't get me wrong, I have no intention of getting back together with him, but, and I know you'll hate me for this, but a small part of me wants to hear what he has to say. It almost feels like I need to see him and ask the things I didn't get to ask. I have all these questions running through my head and sometimes I can't sleep because they keep going round and round my head. Does that make sense?'

'Totally! I've always hated the term *closure*, but I think that's what you need. Remember it's not just about him though, you need to ask him questions, but you also need to give him a piece of your mind. Get it all off your chest. In fact, use it as an opportunity to do just that.'

'Yeah, maybe. I'll think about it. I don't want to make things any worse for myself than they already are. I'm worried that seeing him again will just open up the wounds, which are still pretty raw to be honest.'

'I know. Look you don't have to do anything immediately. Just play it all on your terms. If you decide to see him, just wait until you're good and ready. And if you decide against it, then fine. Just tell him to go stuff it. What do you care after all?'

She did care though, that was the problem.

She didn't hear from him again that week but by the time Friday came round she was thinking about him more than she should. Her moods swung between anger and sadness, and if she'd been feeling angry on that Friday morning, she was almost sure she wouldn't have replied to his email. However, the sadness made her weak and vulnerable. She started thinking back to the Fridays they usually spent together and eventually she caved in.

She stared at the computer screen for what seemed like an age. She made herself a fresh cup of coffee to replace the one which had gone cold as she contemplated her reply. Eventually, she simply typed, *Fine. Come round tonight* and hit the send button before she had any second thoughts.

She didn't give him any alternative date or time. He was lucky she agreed he could come round at all. She didn't check her emails again until five thirty. Mainly because she didn't want to be distracted by his reply, if he replied. And if he hadn't replied, her disappointment would have prevented her from doing any work at all today, and she could ill afford to lose a day's writing.

106

To her astonishment there was an email from him. She took a deep breath and opened it, hands trembling as she did so. It read, *Great. See you about seven thirty. Mack x*

She half hoped he wouldn't have seen it, couldn't make it or had just changed his mind.

She made no effort to get ready. She didn't want to give him the impression she was looking forward to seeing him or this meeting was going to lead to anything. Nevertheless, she was nervy and jittery. Waves of nausea passed over her from time to time, probably the result of a lack of food and too much coffee.

She jumped at the sound of the doorbell. She had an impulse to run into her room and hide, but she knew she had no choice. She had asked for this.

They stood and stared at each other. 'Hi,' Mack said in a gruff voice. He noticed how pale and gaunt she looked. Her eyes were puffy and red, as if she'd been crying.

'God Abbi...' he hesitated, taking a small step forward, unsure if she was going to allow him to come in. As if reading his thoughts, she stepped to the side, allowing him into the hall.

'You'd better go through.' She couldn't bring herself to look him in the eye, but she caught her breath as she watched him walk into the living room, his familiar, broad back and slim hips evoking strong memories and a longing to touch him.

He stood awkwardly not knowing what to do. He could see her tears welling up. 'Abbi,' he said, moving swiftly towards her and taking her in his arms before she could protest, 'I'm so sorry. I didn't mean for any of this to happen.'

Damn! She hadn't meant to cry in front of him. Of all the scenarios she considered in her mind, she didn't think she would cry. She felt his arms wrap around her and she was powerless to resist. She wanted to lose herself in him and pretend the rest had never happened. She felt his lips on hers and before she knew it she was returning his kisses. They lurched over to the sofa, dropping onto it as they removed their clothes. Her mind was blank, concentrating only on the feeling of Mack's hands moving urgently over her body.

In Mack's case, it was a split second decision, the wrong decision in hindsight. He saw the tears and for the briefest of seconds thought of turning on his heels and hot tailing it back to Jen, but he couldn't do that to her. She looked like a wounded puppy and his protective instincts came into play. Before he knew it, he had her in his arms, breathing in her familiar scent. He felt his lips cover hers and he was gone, lost in the moment.

Afterwards, he tried pulling her in close but she jumped up quickly, covering herself up whilst reaching for her clothes.

'For fucks sake Mack, what have we done? That wasn't why I agreed to you coming round. Do you think you can just waltz back in here and it'll all be OK? Do you have any idea what you've done? You have a girlfriend somewhere, who you've been with for years apparently, and then you drag me into the whole thing, totally against my will. You gave me absolutely no choice in it, and just in case you don't know, if I did have a choice, I would have said *No*.' She slumped onto the sofa, picking up Mack's clothes and throwing them at him. 'Get dressed,' she hissed.

Mack pulled his clothes on in silence. He looked at her sitting there, hurt and dejected. 'Abbi… I.'

'Don't,'

'Do you want me to go?'

She shrugged. 'It's up to you.'

'I don't want to go. I wanted to see you, see how you are, apologise. I didn't mean for us to…you know, have sex. It just happened, sorry.'

'How many things can you be sorry for? Why Mack,' she asked with an air of desperation which cut through him.

He leaned forward, resting his forearms on his thighs, 'I wish I knew. I don't know why. I do know I never meant to hurt you or Jen,' he said tentatively.

'Oh yeah, mustn't forget Jen. You're just so thoughtful, not wanting to hurt either of us. How did she take all this?'

Mack felt himself blanche. He hadn't told Jen! He had no intention of telling her and was shocked that Abbi thought he would. 'I eh..'

'She doesn't know and she'll never know if it's up to you. Right?'

'I don't know, no, I don't want to hurt her either.'

She gave him a sidelong glance and her heart lurched. She hated what he'd done to her, but she loved him. She couldn't bear the thought of him not being around. They sat in silence for what seemed like an age. Part of her desperately wanted to know everything, but something inside her was almost warning her off seeking the truth. She suspected it might not be what she wanted to hear.

Finally, she announced she was going to bed. She didn't ask him to join her but she didn't ask him to leave either. She really had no idea what she wanted him to do, so in the end she left him to make up his own mind. If he was still here in the morning, maybe that would tell her something.

She lay in bed, tense and motionless, straining to hear, listening for some kind of clue as to what he might be doing. She was convinced she would hear the door closing and that would be it. Eventually, she fell asleep. Her body jerked as she woke suddenly. The room was in darkness and it took her a moment to realise where she was and what had gone before. She was aware of Mack lying behind her, close, but not touching. His breathing was deep and steady, a sure sign that he was asleep, but he was *here*. He'd decided to stay. He was truly here, in her bed. Surely that must count for something? *How the hell could he be fast asleep though?* As if nothing had happened, when here she was, wide awake, fretting, worrying and wondering what it all meant. *Hadn't it even occurred to him to wake her up and explain what was going on?* Still, she thought, the fact that he was here must mean that he does love her and wants to be together. She smiled to herself, allowing herself to let a tiny piece of happiness to seep through the otherwise dark gloom which for the most part, still engulfed her.

Sleep was clearly going to elude her and as she lay in the dark she slowly began to build a theory of what must have happened. Mack was probably at a point where things with Jen weren't good. Perhaps the relationship was coming to an end, they were probably on the brink of splitting up when she'd met him. Perhaps it was a bit of a messy spilt, or he was trying to spare Jen's feelings. It would be particularly hard on Jen if he announced he'd met someone else. That would just rub salt into the wound.

She began to feel a little calmer as she came to the conclusion that perhaps this wasn't even really Mack's fault, let alone hers. He couldn't help it if things weren't good between himself and Jen or that he'd met someone else by chance.

She pressed her body into his and felt him stir, momentarily, before settling back into his sleep. She moved her hand back and let it rest gently on his thigh, hoping it would be enough to wake him. He slipped his hand around her waist and snuggled closer to her. She lay still for a moment, but realised he was still sleeping. She moved her hand slowly up his thigh and reaching the top, took him in her hand and massaged him gently at first until she felt him come to life. She turned around to face him as she felt him become more aroused. She found his lips with her mouth and pressed them to his. He moaned drowsily before waking up with a start.

He tried to talk but she pushed her mouth harder onto his. She felt his hands move up her thighs, gasping as he reached the top, stroking her gently.

'That feels good,' she whispered, 'don't stop.'

He pressed his fingers firmly against her, making her groan. She wrapped her legs around him, pulling him on top of her. She pushed her body up to meet his as he moved inside her, gripping the top of her thighs tightly, anchoring himself to her. He moved slowly, almost teasing her. He knew she wanted him to move quicker, but he had no intention of doing so. He withdrew from her, making her gasp and squirm, 'No,' she said breathlessly, 'don't stop!' She almost sounded annoyed.

He moved his head down, kissing her breasts and circling them lightly with his tongue. He continued down, tracing his tongue lightly over her stomach and hips, before reaching the top of her thighs, where he hesitated. He could sense she was holding her breath, desperately waiting to feel his warm mouth on her.

He flicked his tongue around her, making her squirm, pushing herself up towards him. She clenched his hair in her hands trying to pull him down onto her, but he resisted, waiting until she was least expecting it.

111

She made small gasping noises, relaxing slightly, letting herself enjoy the feel of the tiny movements he was making, when suddenly, he thrust his tongue deep inside her, causing her to throw her head back and push her pelvis up to meet him, crying out loudly as she did so.

She moved her body into a sitting position and watched in fascination as she saw the top of his dark hair move slowly, feeling the ripples of pleasure run through her with every movement. She wrapped her legs around his head, moaning ecstatically, preparing to give way to the growing desire inside her, when he stopped and moved his body up to meet her, pushing her thighs open and thrusting hard inside her. He pinned her arms over her head as he continued to move quickly, forcing the breath from her with every move.

She gave way to building pleasure, letting it spread down through her pelvis and over her thighs, gasping as she did so. She felt Mack tense as he thrust deeper, eventually letting go with a moan.

They lay there in the darkness, gasping and clutching each other, both absorbed momentarily in their own thoughts.

Mack spoke first, 'Abbi... I,' He was about to explain that this was a mistake and perhaps he should go, but she stopped him.

'Shh,' she said, placing her fingers over his lips, 'It's ok, it's all going to be ok.' She reached up and kissed him slowly, wrapping her arms around him. He lay back and sighed as she curled up and lay against him, stroking his chest gently. She fell into a deep sleep but this time it was Mack who lay awake for the remainder of the night.

He could see the clock out of the corner of his eye. He didn't want to move for fear of waking her. Seven am. His first urge was to run. If he could have slipped out unnoticed, he would have, but she was still curled up against him, one hand lying heavily across his chest. He felt trapped, literally and metaphorically.

He hadn't planned on this happening. His intention had been to apologise and walk away. He was confused by her reaction. She had gone from anger to forgiveness in less than twenty four hours and try as he might, he couldn't fathom it. He had expected her to shout and scream and throw him out, and that would have been the end of it, but he had a slight unease about her reaction.

She stirred, and feeling him next to her, she moved her hand up his chest, and threw her leg over his, rubbing herself against him.

He wanted to resist, but it was difficult. He laughed halfheartedly, 'Sorry, look, I'd better go.'

She was on top of him before he could protest further. He could have thrown her off obviously, but he didn't feel comfortable using his strength to force her off. He did his best not to enjoy it. It was the least he could do.

Once she'd finished, he waited a few moments, as long as was polite, before he headed to the shower. His overwhelming instinct was to go as quickly as possible, but she arrived, at the bathroom door, smiling, holding out a coffee. 'Just how you like it.'

'Eh... thanks, that's great, although I won't stop.' He looked at her apologetically.

'That's ok, you never do.' She watched him intently as he dried himself.

She had that sad, melancholy look on her face, which had drawn him in the first place. It was a look which tugged at his heart strings and made him want to reassure her and make it alright. He reached out and pulled her into him.

113

'I'm sorry,' he sighed, 'I never meant for any of this to happen. Most of all I didn't mean to hurt you.'

She believed him. She could tell by the look on his face that no matter what, he did care for her. She could feel tears roll down her cheeks.

'Shhh, come on, don't cry. It'll be fine.'

He could feel her hot tears against the bare skin of his chest as he held her tight. He was aware he was digging a hole for himself rather than clawing his way out, but he just didn't know what else to say or do. He had come here to end it and he knew he should have walked away last night or this morning but he didn't have it in him to be cruel or harsh, and there lay his problem. Basically he wasn't really cut out to be an adulterer, but somehow he now found himself in the thick of it, building layer upon layer of lies.

***

And so they continued for a few months, picking up where they left off, as if nothing had really changed. Abbi somehow managing to persuade herself that Mack would eventually leave Jen, and Mack, convincing himself that eventually Abbi would be the one to call it a day. Rather, he hoped that's what would happen.

As much as they carried on in the same way, underneath, they both knew things had changed. Mack felt more beholden to her which subtletychanged the dynamics between them. He could tell though that she wasn't entirely happy and was often quieter and more moody.

She was in a particularly quiet mood one evening as they both stared at the television, neither really concentrating, when she came straight out and asked him.

'When do you plan on leaving her?'

Mack was stunned and it clearly showed.

'I eh, I hadn't really thought,' he said lamely.

'Clearly! I'm assuming she does know about us?'

Mack shook his head slowly. He didn't like the way this conversation was heading.

'What?' she asked, horrified. 'Mack, please tell me you've told her. What the hell is going on? Why is it OK for me to know and have to put up with knowing that not only do you have a girlfriend, but that I'm complicit in all of this, but it's somehow not OK for her to know? Maybe she'd be ok with it but I'm not. I don't think I deserve that, do you?' There was a harsh and bitter tone to her voice. 'No,' he shook his head slowly, 'Sorry.'

'Sorry! Sorry! Sorry!' she screamed, 'You're always so fucking sorry Mack, but sorry is just not good enough . We can't go on like this. I feel like I'm putting my life on hold, waiting to see which way you turn. I feel tense and nervous around you, scared to ask you where you see things heading with us, *if* you see things going anywhere , scared to plan anything or suggest we do anything. Don't you see? I can't make any long term plans, either on my own or with you. Unlike you, I can't imagine seeing anyone else while you're still around, so as harsh as it might sound, I might be missing out on the opportunity of meeting someone else because I'm hanging about waiting on you, hoping you might see some sort of future with me, waiting to see if you do, and all of that makes me sound so pathetic and needy that I'm beginning to hate myself for it.

'I know, I can see that, but please, don't hang about on my part.'

She looked at him in shock. 'Don't hang about on my part? Oh my god, you are completely unbelievable. You make it sound like we're organising a night out, which you may or may not turn up to. Jesus Mack you're an insensitive bastard sometimes. It's not that easy! I can't have feelings for two people at the same time. Obviously that's too difficult for you to comprehend though.'

Chapter 5
Mack

He came to realise he didn't like conflict or confrontation, and ultimately, that was probably his downfall. Rather than face things head on, he buried his head in the sand, hoping it would all go away.

He wanted to shoosh her, tell her it would all be OK and sweep it under the carpet, hoping that would put an end to it for now, but he knew they were beyond that, and the inevitably difficult conversations would have to start sometime soon.

'Look, it's not that easy, I can't just leave her.'

'Do you even plan to leave her though? I don't think you do.'

'I... eh, Jesus Abbi. I don't know anything anymore. I feel like you're backing me into a corner, trying to force me into doing something I'm not ready to do yet. I can't do this right now. It's no good. Sorry Abbi.'

That was probably the most decisive thing he'd actually said so far, and even then, it was still fairly bland and non-committal.

Abbi sat stunned. She couldn't believe Mack was turning this around, implying this was her fault.

She watched in astonishment as Mack gathered up his car keys from the table in front of him and left.

He thought that would be the last time he'd see her, and as much as he loved her and would miss her hugely, he couldn't deny that he felt a huge sense of relief. That was it. Done. Over, As easy as that.

Now that it was all over he started to think about it in more depth, wondering how he could have been such an idiot. He thought back to the moment their relationship had intensified. He felt like he'd done his best to avoid having sex with Abbi. He wondered if on some subconscious level he thought it was somehow acceptable as long as they didn't have sex. Certainly, he felt like things had moved to another level and he had a distinctly uneasy feeling about it.

In truth, if he could have turned back time, he would have. He would have resisted her advances, he told himself. He knew from the moment he walked into the kitchen that night that something was different. Something had shifted. Abbi seemed different somehow and looking back he was certain she planned to have sex that night. All the signs were there but he buried the thought. If he was honest, he hadn't expected her to take such an active role in initiating the sex, so he felt he was fairly safe for a while. Although they hadn't had any in depth conversations about relationships he knew she hadn't had that much experience with men. He also had a feeling she might be a little old fashioned, and that, combined with a lack of confidence led him to assume, wrongly, that she would probably wait for him to take the lead.

She had taken him by surprise and he knew it would look odd if he'd turned on his heels and left or wriggled out of having sex, which would have led to questions about *what was wrong?* or *why didn't he want to have sex?* He didn't have an answer to any of that, so in the end it was easier to just go along with it.

Not that he didn't enjoy it. He'd had a hard job holding back, and in some ways it was easy to just let go and let it happen, until he looked at her properly and realised, with a jolt that it wasn't Jen. There was a moment when he almost pushed her off, pulled up his jeans and bolted, but the moment passed and he gave in, willingly.

There was no going back after that. Someone, he couldn't remember who, had said that once you'd had sex, it was difficult, if not impossible to go back to holding hands. So in other words, be sure you were doing the right thing.

Abbi obviously enjoyed it and was keen to spend most of her time in bed with Mack, which, he reflected, probably made the affair easier. They hardly ever went out so he had less chance of getting caught.

All in all, he concluded, life had a strange way of making the whole thing easy for him. Too easy. In his less lucid moments, he totally blamed fate and circumstances. If there was a chance they could have been caught, he would have ended it sooner, he reasoned with himself. If the sex hadn't been so good, Abbi would have become bored staying in. If she had been more demanding of his time, or insisted he stayed over more often, that would have backed him into a corner sooner, and perhaps it would have all become too difficult for him and he would have been forced to end it, rather than just having a passive role in the whole thing.

In the end though, he unwittingly found himself leading two lives and somehow getting away with it all, without even meaning to.

Little did he know he hadn't gotten away with it. The last thing he expected was Abbi to turn up on his doorstep. He was pretty sure she didn't even know where he lived. He had been stupid and naïve to think he could just put it all behind him and carry on as normal, as if none of it had ever happened.

***

He sighed to himself as he sipped his beer. He wasn't convinced all this soul searching and reflection was good for himHe didn't know what normal was anymore and if someone had put a gun to his head and forced him to make a decision one way or the other, he knew he would falter, if even just for a second. The feelings he had for Abbi took him by surprise. But did they match his feelings for Jen? He couldn't tell any more. His head was a mess.

For now though, he felt he had made a decision and taken action, which as hard as it was, it felt like he'd done the right thing.

Chapter 6
Mack

The weeks turned to months and he finally accepted the inevitable, that there would be no response. He had written a few more letters, ten to be precise, called her mobile and landline, waited for her outside the flat, but there had been no contact since that Sunday. It was as if she had just vanished into thin air.

With a heavy heart, he reluctantly accepted it was over. His father was right. He was still alive. Life carried on around him. His broken heart was slowly healing as long as he didn't think about her and the life he'd thrown away.

Life seemed slower now. He just seemed to plod along, getting through every day rather than sprinting towards some unknown finish line. He moved in with friends and slowly started to rebuild the pieces of his life. Work continued, he picked up his football again and even managed a few nights out with friends. It wasn't the same. His sense of fun had diminished and he felt less carefree, but it was tolerable, and that was perhaps as good as he could expect.

Chapter 7

Mack Five Years Later

'Thanks for agreeing to meet me, I know you didn't have to,' he said nervously, running his hands through his hair.

She eyed him suspiciously. This was harder than she expected and she questioned whether it had been a wise move, not even sure herself of her own underlying reasons. She reminded herself that she had no option though. There was a reason she needed to see him. Their coffee arrived, and she wondered what the waitress made of the frosty silence between them. She stirred hers, afraid to actually take a sip in case her hands shook and gave away how nervous she felt.

He looked at her, pleadingly. She knew he was feeling uncomfortable but she had no intention of making this easy for him. She waited until he spoke.

'I... er... God, where do I start? I've thought of nothing else but her since I bumped into you... and you, obviously,' he added nervously.

She immediately put her hand up to stop him. This isn't about us, please don't make any mention of us. This is just about Lily.'

'OK, OK, sorry, it's just...' he gave a heavy sigh, 'Ok, let's just talk about her. There's so much I want to ask, about her, about what happened, when you…. you know, what happened when you found out. I can't bear to think of you on your own, I should have been there.'

'Yes, you should have, but you made your choice. Whatever happened was all your doing and you'll have to live with that for the rest of your life. I can't say I have any sympathy for you, so don't go looking for any.'

'No… I… I wasn't, sorry, I was just saying.' They sat in silence again for a few moments. 'When did you find out?'

'A few months after I left Edinburgh.'

'You left Edinburgh?'

'Yes, what did you think had happened to me? Yes, I left, I needed to get away from any chance of bumping into you and from the humiliation and stupidity I felt every day when I woke up in the bed we had shared. I went to Devon.'

'Devon?'

'Yes, Devon, to stay with my cousin. I managed to get a job in one of the labs at the university.'

'A bit of a come down for you wasn't it?'

'It was better than nothing. Beggars can't be choosers and all that and what with my change of circumstances, I had no choice. Obviously they couldn't give me any permanent work, but they were good to me. When Lily came along, my parents moved down to help me out.'

'They moved?' he looked shocked.

'Yes, they moved. They didn't feel they had much choice. You see, your actions didn't just affect me, they had an impact on those around me as well. And it's not just then or the here and now that's affected. You ruined any chance I might have of finding someone else. It would have been difficult enough meeting someone else as it was, but having

Lily made it impossible. I'd have to trust them with Lily. They'd have to love her as much as I do, and they'd have to settle for second best.'

He looked at her through confused eyes, 'you mean…?'

'No! I don't mean second best to you! I mean second best to Lily. It's hard to understand if you don't have children, but when you do have them, you love them instinctively and fiercely. You'd do anything to protect them, it's almost an animal instinct. I can't explain, but your child becomes your number one priority and everything else comes after, so any man I meet would never be my number one. I imagine if both parents are around and together, they both feel the same, so they both naturally accept they're second best and don't think much of it. I can't imagine trusting anyone enough to let them in. I'd be taking too much of a risk that they'd hurt her as well as me.'

He hung his head and shook it heavily, 'I'm so sorry. I'll never be able to say that often enough for it to make any difference to what's happened, but I am deeply sorry.'

She shrugged. 'You're right, it'll never help. Anyway,' she continued with her story, 'My dad managed to get a transfer and my mum took a sabbatical to come down and be with me, to help me out and to be with Lily. I got a permanent job at the university and then a research post in The States.'

'The States! America?' he looked shocked.

'Yes, The States, do you have to repeat everything I say?'

'It's just that…. you really must have wanted to get as far away from me as possible.'

'It wasn't all about you at that point,' she said coldly, 'I needed to do something for me and for Lily. I was thinking of her future. You see, it changes you, motherhood. You realise that there's no room for being selfish, everything is about your child.'

'Yes, yes, of course. Are you back now? For good I mean?'

'Yes, I came back six months ago. I want Lily to go to school here and I want her to know my family properly, so I'm back now. I've got a job at the University here. It's not what I ever wanted to do, but I can't complain. What I want isn't important any longer.'

'Right,' he paused. 'I've thought a lot about her. I've thought about nothing else actually. I know this is too early, but if there's any chance, I really want to be a part of her life.'

She knew she needed to keep her guard up. If Mack saw any chink in her armour he'd be right in there, trying to break down her defenses.

'Well, you're right about one thing, it is way too early to think about that. I'm not stupid, I know that's why you wanted to meet me.'

He opened his mouth to speak, to protest that he was also here to see her as well, but she raised her hand again to stop him.

'There's a lot to think about. I need to do what's best for Lily. I know I shouldn't deny her the right to get to know her real father, but, and it's a big but, I need to weigh that up with everything else that can go wrong. What if you exit her life as quickly as you enter it? That's a huge risk, not just to her immediate feelings but her whole emotional stability for the rest of her life, and I don't know if I can risk that.'

The burning question etched on her brain though was one she couldn't mention. What if *he* met someone else, got married, had other children? Where would Lily fit in then? Mack might think that was manageable, but another woman might not. She had cast her eye over his left hand and didn't see any ring, or an indent where there might have been one, but that didn't rule out the possibility that he had a partner or girlfriend. And if he did, or if he met someone and got married, how would she feel? She knew, even after all these years it would still hurt like hell. She also knew though that she couldn't let this be the main reason for stopping him seeing Lily. That would be selfish. Perhaps this was the ultimate sacrifice she would have to make as a mother.

She had spoken to her mother and sister about it, but they hadn't really been able to offer much help. Her mother's first instinct had been that she should have nothing to do with him, but eventually she came round and felt that perhaps she needed to consider it.

He broke into her thoughts. 'Have you told her about me?'

She sighed, taking a sip of her lukewarm coffee. 'Not in the way you'd want. I've tried to be truthful and honest with her but there are some things that a four year old brain can't understand. When she asked if I knew where you were I said *No*, because I didn't, although I'm sure I could have found you if I'd tried, but what do I say to her when she asks if you were nice, if you were handsome? *Yes, your daddy was nice, he was handsome and lovely and we loved each other and we hardly ever argued and I thought we'd be together forever. That was the plan.* None of that would make sense to her. You see, other single parents have a really good reason why they're single, but I don't. How can she make sense of the fact that you meet someone, you fall

126

in love, you both love each other, you have a baby and then you don't stay together? What message will that give her?'

She knew now she was getting into dangerous territory as she was beginning to talk about herself.

Mack looked increasingly uncomfortable. 'I can see it's all been really difficult for you.'

'Yes, it was bloody hard! All of it, but ironically, I wouldn't change things, because if I did, I wouldn't have Lily and she's all that matters now. Yes, I would have preferred her to have a stable family life, to have a mum and dad who love her, of course I would want that part to be different, but it's not and I can't change that, so there's no point going over it.'

'I do love her,' he raised his voice in protest, but she silenced him again.

'How can you, you haven't even met her, you don't know her,' although underneath, she was pretty certain he would love her, given the chance. How could he not? She was very like him, partly in looks, but more in character. She saw Mack every single day of her life when she saw her daughter, which made life harder, but not one she would change.

'No, I know that, but I can't explain it. The moment I saw her I knew she was mine and I was smitten. She's beautiful, like you.'

She stared at him. Hand on heart, he hadn't changed a bit. He was still as handsome and youthful looking. There were no lines, no grey hairs. No signs of weariness or fatigue brought on by sleepless nights and an energy sapping toddler who was constantly on the go. She knew the same couldn't be said of her. She bore all the hallmarks of motherhood. Eyes that always looked tired, hair that was quickly pulled back into a knot behind her neck, and a face that had no trace of makeup.

She knew he was being kind. In actual fact, she thought Lily looked more like Mack. She often wondered how she would have coped if she'd given birth to a boy. A mini version of Mack, but as it turned out, her daughter was exactly that, just without the Y chromosome.

'I've no doubt you would love her Mack, but you could also hurt her and that's what I need to think about. If I let you meet her and be part of her life, the terms need to be crystal clear.'

He almost leapt up. His eyes brightened and he straightened in his chair. 'Yes! They would be, absolutely, anything you say. Whatever the terms I'll stick to them. *If!* You said *if.* That means you must be considering it?'

*Damn!*She had let her defenses down and he'd grabbed the chance, as she knew he would.

'Look Mack, it really is a big *if*, I can't promise anything this big at the moment. I really need time to think about it on my own, without you pressurising me. I need to think what's best for Lily, do you understand that?'

'Yes,' he said reluctantly. 'I do. Do you have any photos of her?' he asked more hopefully.

She smiled for the first time since they'd sat down. 'What kind of mother do you think I am? Of course I have photos of her!' She pulled out her phone and started scrolling through them. Mack was hanging over her, telling her to stop every time she tried to move to the next one. He gazed longingly at each one, reluctant to move onto the next. Eventually, she handed him the phone. She wasn't comfortable being in such close proximity to him. He had exactly the same smell, which only served to evoke powerful and painful memories.

'I… I hope you don't mind, but I told my mum about her,' he looked across at her with a worried expression.

She shrugged. 'It's up to you what you do. I can't stop you. What did they say?'

'It was just my mum. I think my dad would take it pretty badly. She…. what did she say? God, where do I start? She burst into tears, she tried to hit me, she was so angry and pissed off at me because of the mess I'd made of everything, angry because she'd missed out on her granddaughter and might still never see her,' he stopped, looking across at her hopefully, for some trace of understanding.

'Stop Mack, don't try the emotional blackmail. I've already been through it in my own mind, the fact that Lily is missing out on her other grandparents, aunties and uncles, a whole family who would shower her with love, so you don't need to remind me of all of that. I need time and space to think it all through. It's such a big decision to make. I can't afford to get it wrong,'

He nodded, indicating he understood that, at least. He bowed his head for a moment but when he looked up, there was a pleading look in his eyes. 'Look, I know this is a big ask, but would you mind sending me a few photos, just so I can show my mum?'

She nodded. As much as she hated Mack for the hurt he'd caused her, she wasn't heartless. She knew how her own mother would feel if she knew Lily existed and couldn't see her. She sent him four photos from her phone. 'I'll send you more of her baby photos when I get back to the house.'

He nodded, hanging his head again. She had the feeling he was close to tears, but he regained his composure and looked directly at her, with his dark brown puppy dog eyes.

'Thanks. I can't thank you enough. It means so much…' he tailed off.

She could tell he was choked. 'Look, I have to go. My mum's got Lily but I need to get back. I promised I'd take her to the beach later. She's desperate to use her new bucket and spade.' That did it, she could clearly see tears in his eyes. He got up quickly and brushed his hands over his eyes.

'I'll pay the bill,' he said gruffly, walking up to the counter. She wasn't sure what to do next. It didn't feel right just to walk off, but it would be just as awkward walking out with him. What would they do when they got outside? He was back at her side before she had a chance to make a decision.

Once outside, he turned to her, 'So, would it be OK to contact you again?'

'Look, I'm not going to spin this out. I'll make a decision and get in touch to let you know OK? I'll mail you some photos over tonight if I'm not too tired. If I don't do it tonight, I'll do it tomorrow and then we can arrange to meet again, OK?'

'Yeah, Ok,' he smiled, looking hopeful. He hesitated, as if to move towards her, but stopped himself. She'd never seen him this hesitant, this unsure of himself. She checked herself. She didn't want to feel any sympathy for him. She didn't want to have any feelings for him.

'I met her you know, a few weeks, maybe three or four, after we… well after everything that happened.'

'You met up? With… Why?' he looked genuinely shocked.

She shrugged, 'Not sure really. It seemed like the right thing to do. I thought it might give me some answers or… well, I don't know what. I'm not sure it helped me at all.'

She wanted to ask if Mack had seen her again and what happened in the aftermath, but she didn't. She knew this would open up old wounds and be another chink in her armour. 'I'll be in touch, OK? She said quickly, before there could be any more conversation.

She decided to walk home. It was only twenty minutes away so she'd be back in plenty time to take Lily to the beach but she really needed some time on her own to gather her thoughts. Time alone was a precious commodity. It was such a rare occurrence that even twenty minutes alone was a luxury.

She could feel his eyes upon her as she walked away from the café. Today had been hard. She could feel old wounds open up and she could quite conceivably unravel if she let herself. She took a deep breath and kept walking. *One step at a time* she told herself. Rather than try to gather her thoughts and come to some decision about what she was going to do, she found herself casting her mind back four years or so. He'd asked her what had happened when she'd found out she was pregnant, and in truth, the whole thing was hazy, which was another reason she resented him.

Chapter 8

She'd always wanted children, but had imagined it would be a planned and happy time. She imagined they'd find out together. She'd pictured them, buying the kit, doing the test and looking at the results together, keeping it secret, going for scans, telling friends and family the happy news. She'd do all the right things. Mack would read all the books, guide her through it, make sure she took her vitamins come to ante-natal classes with her. She would look after herself, watch her bump growing, place Mack's hand on her swollen tummy when the baby was kicking…. None of that happened.

She was in such a state that she didn't even notice anything was amiss. She literally retreated into a shell, eating only when she remembered or when her cousin insisted. She was always slim, and could ill-afford to lose weight, but she became scrawny in a matter of weeks. She didn't sleep, didn't eat and was barely functioning. Thank God for her cousin, Elle, who looked after her and nurtured her, forcing her to eat and drink where she could. It was actually Elle who first suggested she might be pregnant. Elle walked in on her one day as she was getting dressed and stopped, taken aback, as she caught sight of her. She hadn't looked at herself for months. She knew she probably looked terrible but didn't expect that reaction. 'What?' she asked, perplexed.

'Eh, well don't take this the wrong way, but have you looked at yourself recently?' Elle asked carefully.

'No,' she snorted, 'what's the point? I know I probably look like shit, but who's caring?'

'Well, I could be wrong but I thought your stomach was always sickeningly flat, and now it's eh… not.'

She slowly turned and looked at herself side on in the mirror. It took a few moments for it to sink in. She gasped, her hands flying to her mouth. 'Fuck me! No! It can't be,' she said running her hand over her stomach. 'How?' she said in a whisper.

'You really had no idea?'

She shook her head in disbelief. She didn't think it was possible to look and feel more miserable than she already did, but it was. She felt the air being sucked from her lungs as she stumbled to reach the bed. 'What am I going to do?' she asked, more to herself than to Elle. She sat down on the edge of the bed with a thump and stared down at the tiny bulge, all the more obvious because of her diminished size.

Elle sat down next to her and rubbed her arm gently. 'Look, first things first, let's get you an appointment with the doctor, and then you can think about what you're going to do.'

She nodded her head, lost for words.

'I'll go and call the doctor and then I'm going to prepare you some breakfast, which you ARE going to eat, no arguing.'

Elle left the room to allow her get dressed in privacy. *How on earth could she not have noticed?* She thought back to recent months and weeks. The way she'd been feeling, it was quite plausible it could have escaped her notice. She'd felt tired and slightly queasy but she put all that down to lack of sleep and lack of food. *Of course, perhaps she wasn't pregnant, perhaps there was some other explanation, s*he thought hopefully.

Elle came back with a tray of food, the very sight of which made her feel nauseous. 'Elle, I don't think I…'

Elle held up her hand, 'Let's just take it easy. I'm not asking you to eat all of this, but just take small mouthfuls to begin with, and see what you can manage, OK?' Elle gave her most re-assuring smile, but it was obvious she was worried.

She did her best to eat some of the food in front of her. She knew if she was pregnant, that she'd have to start eating and drinking properly.

'I've managed to get an emergency appointment with the doctor tomorrow, so try to get some rest and not to worry too much until then. You look exhausted, why don't I call your work and let them know you're not well, and you can maybe go back to bed for a few hours.'

There was nothing that she'd like more, but she was just helping out in the labs and if she didn't work, she didn't get paid. 'No, its fine thanks. There's no point in me hanging around doing nothing. I'd be better to go to work and take my mind off it.'

The next few months passed in a whirlwind of anxiety and turmoil. She wouldn't have believed it possible to cry more than she had done when she and Mack split up, but it seemed she had a shedload more tears to cry.

The first tears were for herself. *Hadn't she suffered enough? Why was this happening? Was someone trying to punish her?* Her next batch of tears were brought on by guilt. Guilt that she resented this baby and that her first thoughts were for herself. Finally, she cried out of worry and fear. *How was she going to cope with a baby on her own?*

Elle was a rock. She was there for her every day and helped her through crisis after crisis. According to the midwife, she had probably conceived around the time she and Mack had split up. This truly was someone having one big gigantic laugh at her expense.

In the end though, pregnancy was possibly the best thing to have happened to her. It forced her out of her state of shock and the downward spiral of self-neglect she was in and gave her something to focus on. With Elle's help, she pulled herself together and busied herself with preparations for the baby's arrival. She wasn't due for months and had only had the one scan so far, but she needed to regain some control. Her Aunt Shonagh, Elle's mother, lived in a spacious cottage all by herself, ever since Elle's father had died a few years ago. Aunt Shonagh very generously insisted that she came to stay at the cottage when the baby was born, for as long as she needed. She had often said the place was too big and too quiet for her, filled with too many memories, but she was reluctant to give it up, as it was the family home for Elle and her two brothers. Having a baby in the house would bring it to life again and give her something to do. She could help out whenever she was needed. It would be like having a live-in nanny she joked, although at this point there wasn't much to laugh about.

***

She was pulled back into the present moment by squeals of 'Mummy, mummy, you're back. Where have you been?'

Her daughter came racing down the hall and threw her arms around her, hugging her as tightly as a four year old could.'

'I've only been gone an hour,' she laughed, kissing the top of her head.

'I know, but what if the sun goes away and it's too cold to go to the beach?'

'It's never too cold to go to the beach, but look,' she said opening the door, 'the sun is definitely shining. I think it'll even be warm enough for an ice-cream. Come on, let's go before everyone else has the same idea and all the ice-cream's gone.'

'Hang on,' her mother shouted, 'I'll come with you.'

'How did it go?' her mother asked, as they walked along the beach, watching Lily dart back and forward, running away from the waves screeching with excitement, as they chased her onto the dry beach. Sometimes they caught her, lapping around her ankles, and sometimes she escaped their icy clutches. Even at the height of summer, the North Sea was never warm.

'Whew,' she exhaled slowly. 'Hard. Where do I start? I knew what he wanted so that part wasn't a great surprise, but just seeing him again, talking to him,' she looked down at the sand, trying hard to keep control of her emotions.

'Just take your time love,' her mother said, placing a hand on her arm and giving it a gentle squeeze.

'What? Do you mean telling you what happened or making a decision?' she laughed.

'Both. You don't have to tell me about your meeting today, or ever, but if it helps, you know I'm here. As for your decision, well, it's exactly that. It's your decision, and we'll know what it is to be soon enough, but neither your father nor I will interfere. We've discussed it.'

She looked up, surprised. 'God, that was quick.'

'We spoke about it the day you mentioned you'd met him. We knew what was coming and that it would be hard, no matter what, but that's life. Life is hard and cruel sometimes. It's part of being an adult. Learning to deal with whatever life throws at you and making the best of it.'

'What would you do mum?'

'I knew you'd ask me that but it doesn't matter what I'd do. This is about you and what you feel is the best. I know it's a tough decision but you must make it yourself, otherwise it might never feel like your own, and I think it's important that it does. You'll do what's best for Lily though, no matter the cost to yourself, I know that,' she smiled reassuringly at her daughter.

They were interrupted by Lily racing across the sand, dark hair flapping out like a kite behind her. Her dark brown eyes were wide with happiness and excitement. 'I've just seen a bigger boy with the most awesome ice-cream. Can I have one like that, please, please mummy.'

'Ok,' she smiled, 'let's go see what we can do.'

Later that evening once Lily was in bed, she began to tidy up. She longed to just flop onto the sofa with a glass of wine, but those days were gone. This was grown up life, she thought, reflecting on her earlier conversation with her mother.

She fished through her jacket pocket to find her keys and phone and felt a piece of paper. Taking it out, she saw it was folded, but her name was on the front in writing that she recognised instantly. She opened it carefully, not sure she wanted to see what was inside. She was aware of her heart beating faster than normal. She read it slowly, absorbing the words.

I wrote you so many letters in the beginning but ripped most of them up, every one. None of them could truly convey what I was feeling or what I wanted to say. That's because there were no words to explain it, because I didn't know myself. To say I was an idiot wouldn't do it justice. I was more than that. Even then I knew that I'd ruined everything for everyone. I'd let everyone down, but now, with Lily, I can't even begin to describe how much I hate myself for my stupid behavior. For hurting you and missing out on a beautiful daughter. I don't blame you if you hate me and I wouldn't blame Lily either. I know you really didn't want to speak about us today and I understand why, but I just want you to know one thing. I loved you. With all my heart. I still love you. I miss you every single day. There was never really anyone else. It was always you. Mack xx

Tears rolled freely down her cheeks. She made no attempt to stop them because these would be the last tears she ever cried for him. She had cried and cried until she thought it wouldn't be possible to cry any more, but still the tears had kept coming. They had of course eventually dried up, but her heart had ached every day. She felt she'd taken a backwards step as she swiped a hand over her damp cheeks.

She ran her fingers over the words, *there was never really anyone else.*

'But there was though Mack, there was.' She said as she folded the note and put it back in her pocket. She'd made her decision.

***

'If you meet her I'll have to tell her who you are. Do you understand?' she spoke to him as a teacher might to a small child.

'Yes, yes, absolutely, I've no problem with that!' He was almost bursting with excitement.

'No, but she might.'

He looked confused, so she tried to explain in simple terms.

'Look, she hasn't asked about you for a while, so if I tell her that her daddy's here and wants to meet her, she might not be overly excited, I don't know. And if she's not ready or refuses, I have to respect her decision, even though she's only five.'

'Oh,' he said, crestfallen, 'Right, I hadn't thought of that. Do you think she might? Refuse I mean?'

'I have no idea. Really, I'm not just saying that. It's been a topic that's not out of bounds exactly, but I've never brought it up on purpose.'

'Ok. Is there anything I can do that might help?'

She could see the look of desperation on his face. 'I don't know. I have no experience of this. I'm as new to this part as you. I think I just have to bite the bullet and ask her.'

'Ok. When…when do you think you'll do it?'

'Now. When I go back. There's no point in putting it off.'

He nodded. 'God I feel sick. This is worse than anything I've ever felt.'

'Just as well you weren't at the birth then!' she said dryly.

'Don't. I should have been there. It eats away at me every day.' She could see the pain and turmoil behind his

139

eyes but it was no more than he deserved.She got up to go. 'I'll call you as soon as I know.'

He nodded glumly. He didn't appear capable of moving.

***

She was definitely her father's daughter. Her response was instant. Of course she wanted to meet her father!

'When can we meet him? Is he here now? How did you find him?' were amongst the first of many questions she asked, her eyes wide with anticipation.

There was no point in trying to calm her down or suggesting they wait. It would be like asking her to wait a few days before opening her Christmas presents. Lily jumped around her, asking question after question.

'Ok, stop. You need to pause for breath and if you do that I'll call him now.' She was almost as caught up in the excitement as her daughter, until she realised what she was about to do. Her fingers were shaking as she scrolled through her for phone for his number.

Mack answered the phone on the first ring. 'Yes, oh God, is it bad news?'

'No, it's not bad news. Can you meet us now?'

She had to move the phone away from her ear as he yelled and whooped with joy.

'Too fucking right I can. Where?'

'Just as well I didn't have the phone on loud speak. You'll have to watch that.'

'Oh God sorry. I will, I will, I promise.'

Lily studied a photo of Mack en route to meet him at the local park. 'He is the most handsome man I have ever seen. He looks way nicer than anyone else's dad. And look mummy!' she squealed with excitement, 'he has the same colour eyes and hair as me!'

'I know. Crazy eh?' she laughed

Mack was waiting for them when they arrived, anxiously checking everyone who walked towards him. The moment he saw them he raced across. Lily stood for a moment, looking a little nervous and hesitant, which was unlike her, but understandable given the circumstances.

Mack bent down to her level. 'You must be Lily.' He was clearly nervous and looked up, not sure what to do next. He looked back towards Lily, 'I've been so… I'm so happy to meet you at last. You're so beautiful, even more beautiful than the photos.' He was clearly choked.

Lily smiled, hesitantly. She held out the teddy she was carrying. 'This is Winnie the Pooh. He's my favourite bear.'

'Wow! I had one just like him when I was your age. In fact, I still have him. Do you think your Winnie would like to meet mine? Maybe they could be friends?'

She nodded and gave a shy smile, her long lashes framing her perfect oval brown eyes. Identical to Mack's

'So, eh, what do you want to do? I mean, what do you normally do at the park?' he was clearly nervous and on edge.

Lily shrugged and then said tentatively, 'Mummy normally pushes me on the swings.'

'Ok, well I think I can manage that. Would you like me to push you? I must admit I haven't been to the park for a long time. I might have a go on the swings. Do you think mummy might push me if I asked nicely?'

Lilly giggled and looked up, 'would you mummy?', but she shot Mack a look that clearly said, *don't push your luck.*

'Eh, maybe not today. Today it's maybe better that I push you. How high do you like to go?' he said starting to push her slowly as she wriggled onto the seat.

'Into the trees,' she shouted, relaxing a little.

'She'll have you there for hours. I might go and get a coffee. Want one?'

'Yeah, thanks,' he smiled, but his gaze was elsewhere.

Chapter 9

Five Years, Six Months Later

'Mummy, who are you talking to?' Lily shouted from her room?

It was barely eight 'o' clock but she didn't often sleep any longer.

'Oh, eh Daddy.'

'Daddy's here? Already? How long has he been here?' she screeched, indignant that no one had told her. She came racing out of her room, Mack's Winnie the Pooh swinging loosely in her hand. 'Where is he?'

'Oh, eh, he's in my room. He wasn't well last night so I said he could stay over and I slept in the living room.' She didn't know why she felt she had to explain this to a five and a half year old.

Lily ignored her anyway and raced through to the bedroom, jumping on Mack, who was clearly still half asleep. 'Daddy, daddy, why didn't you come and wake me?' She bounced up and down in excitement. 'You look funny in mummy's bed'

'Woah, now that's some welcome.' He wiped his eyes and rubbed his hands through his hair, trying to look bright and alert.

'Mummy says you're ill. Does that mean we can't go to the beach?' Her expression changing in seconds from glee to disappointment.

'What, no? I feel great now. I just needed a good sleep,' he said, looking sheepishly over Lily's shoulder. 'In fact, the beach is just what I need. I might show you some of my surf moves if you're lucky.'

'Mack,' came a warning voice from the doorway.

'Ok, maybe no surf moves today. Maybe my legendary sandcastle building skills. How about that?'

'Ok, I'll go and get my bucket and spade and then can we go, please?'

'Well, yes, in just a minute or two. I need a shower and a coffee, then I'm all yours.' He smiled, patting her head affectionately. 'I tell you what, as it's so early,' he said checking his watch, 'how about you cuddle into me for a wee while and I can read you a story.'

'Ok, I'll get my favourite book,' she said bounding off the bed and through to her room. 'I can't wait to tell everyone at school my daddy stayed the night, but granny and granddad might be worried when I tell them you were ill,' she chirped.

'Oh my God, how do we explain that? I'll leave you to come up with an explanation as to why it wouldn't be a good idea to tell people at the moment, shall I?'

Mack looked a bit stricken. 'Jesus, what do I say? You want me to lie to her, is that what you mean?

'Yes, don't overthink it Mack. It doesn't need to be one of your huge motherfucker lies, just a white lie,' she snapped. She immediately regretted it. 'Sorry,' she sighed, 'I didn't mean that to sound as bad as it did.'

'Come here,' he said, holding out his hand. 'I deserve it and am going to have to get used to it. If you're angry with me it means you still have some feelings for me.' He pulled her down onto the bed and reached his hands behind her neck pressing his forehead to hers. 'I love you. I swear to God I will never hurt you again and I will never hurt Lily. I know you can't believe that right now, and maybe you never will. All I'm asking you for is a chance to prove it.'

He pulled her forward and kissed her. She tried to pull away but he held her tight and continued to kiss her, only the sound of feet running up the corridor made him release her quickly.

'This is what it will be like you know. You won't get any peace. There won't be much time for us to spend together like we used to. Are you prepared for that?'

'Absolutely. One hundred percent,' he grinned.

Lily crashed through the door, oblivious to any intimacy and jumped into the bed, and nestled under his arm. Mack pulled the covers around them and smiled.

'I'll make coffee then shall?' she said, but she was well aware no one was listening to her.

***

Chapter 10

Her hands shook slightly as she picked up the kettle. Her stomach was in knots. She couldn't make up her mind if she was extremely happy or extremely stupid.

What the hell had she done? Whatever she'd done it was all of her own making. She had been the one doing the leading. She wasn't even sure how she'd let Mack get close enough to her to kiss her, let alone do anything else.

It had all happened a few weeks ago. They had been sitting in the garden enjoying the last of the evening sun as Lily slept in bed. They came in when the sun disappeared behind the trees for the night. She had poured more wine for them both as they stood whispering in the kitchen, careful not to wake Lily. That was how it happened, she realised. He'd come over to her as she handed him the glass. He was standing just a little too close, close enough to detect the faint smell of his aftershave. Some sort of sandalwood base, she recalled.

There he was, standing in front of her, in his shorts, t-shirt and bare feet, arms tanned, from hours spent outside in the summer sun, smiling.

Without realising it, she reached over and pulled him towards her, reaching up to kiss him, and it wasn't just a peck. She took him by surprise, that much was clear. But it was a pleasant surprise by the look on his face. He hesitated for a moment before cupping her chin in his hand and returning the kiss.

She pushed her body into his, but she felt him resist. He placed his hands on her hips and pinned her to the kitchen unit, keeping a degree of space between their bodies. She tried to run her hands up his back but he pulled them away, pinning them to his side as he reached in and kissed her again, slowly this time.

'I might not be able to stop myself if you keep doing that,' he placed his forehead on hers and looked down at her.

'Maybe I don't want you to,' she whispered.

He groaned, 'Oh, God, don't say that, please, you don't know what it's doing to me.'

She kissed him again and pulled him towards her. He didn't resist this time. She ran her hand up his shorts.

'Not here,' he whispered.

'OK,' she said, about to lead him through to her bedroom, but he stopped her. 'Are you sure about this?'

She nodded and he followed her through. He closed the door gently. Lily was in the room down the hall but he had no idea if she was a light sleeper. There was so much he didn't know about her he realised, before he turned his attention completely back to the matter in hand.

She pulled him towards the bed and down on top of her and began tugging at his clothes frantically. Mack tried to slow it down. He didn't want this to be a quickie, succumbing to the heat of the moment. He told her later that he wanted her to enjoy it and make sure she wanted to make love rather than just seeking instant gratification.

In actual fact, part of her had just been seeking instant gratification. God knows, it had been years since she'd had sex, but, as much as she hated to admit it, she was glad they had taken their time. He asked her several times if she was sure, if she wanted to stop, even though it would have killed him if she'd said, *yes, stop. This was all a terrible mistake.*

So there it was. She'd started it. She was ninety nine percent sure Mack wouldn't have made the first move. Changed days she thought, biting her bottom lip.

Rather than fall asleep as he used to do, he propped himself up on one elbow, looked down at her and smiled. She couldn't help herself, the tears rolled down her cheeks.

A look of pain and anguish crossed his face. 'Oh baby, don't.' He put his arm around her and pulled her into his chest, stroking her hair gently. 'I'm so sorry. I wish I could take away all the hurt and pain I've caused you. I wish I could turn back time. I wish I wasn't such an asshole.'

'So do I,' she sobbed.

He continued to stroke and whisper soothing words until she fell asleep in his arms.

***

The following week had felt like torture. Mack had been round every evening in some guise or other, either taking Lily to an after school activity, to the park or dropping off a cardigan or hair band she'd left in his car, although there was an awkwardness between them.

There was so much unsaid and neither of them seemed capable of broaching the unspoken subject. They skirted round each other like wary tom cats. Mack maintained some physical contact by way of a light hand on her arm or a peck on the cheek, but nothing more. He couldn't help noticing that she looked miserable.

Eventually he couldn't take the suspense any longer. It was Saturday evening and he knew Lily was at her grandparents for the night, which meant they'd have the place to themselves.

He had butterflies in his stomach as he rang the doorbell. He was practicing his opening line, a bright and breezy, somewhat nonchalant *'Hi,'* or a more serious *'Hi,'* with a look of concern? The door opened before he was ready so it ended up a slightly high pitched, surprised 'Hi.'

She maintained a blank expression. He noticed that she had mastered the art of never making things easy for him these days. She waited expectantly.

He cleared his throat. 'I... eh... thought you might fancy a cheeky wee glass of red while you relax tonight,' he said, holding up a bottle of wine and attempting his best smile.

She held the door open and signaled for him to come in. 'You'll be joining me no doubt,' she said dryly.

'Well, if you're asking,' he smiled, giving her a peck on the cheek before making his way through to the kitchen. She followed him through. She was about to tell him to help himself to the glasses but she saw that he already had. He poured them both a glass and handed one to her, taking a large swig of his own.

She couldn't help but notice that he was staring at his feet, looking slightly uncomfortable. She took a deep breath to steady her nerves. She knew what was coming.

He laced his fingers through hers and cleared his throat. 'Look, I... I don't know what's happened to us this week, but things haven't been right, I do know that, I...' he faltered, 'I want you to be honest with me. Do you have any regrets about last week?'

'Do you?' she spluttered.

149

'I asked first, but no, since you ask.'

She nodded. 'OK.'

'You haven't answered my question,' he pressed anxiously.

She took a moment to reply. 'No, no I don't.'

Mack let out a sigh of relief. 'Thank God for that. You had me worried for a moment. If that's the case can I ask you something else then? Why have you been looking so miserable? Especially after a night of what I thought was spectacularly good sex.'

She took a swipe at him but he blocked her with his hand and pulled her into his arms.

'Do you have to make a joke about everything?' she asked

'Only when I'm nervous. You haven't answered my question. Are you sure you don't any doubts? I mean, I'll be devastated if you do, but it's no more than I deserve.'

She stared at her feet. 'No, I don't have any doubts, but I feel like I should. I feel like I should regret it and I should tell you where to go, but I don't want to. I'm not unhappy, just a bit... I don't know, pissed off with myself I suppose.'

He nodded and opened his mouth to speak but she interrupted, 'and also, well, I wasn't sure if you maybe had been having second thoughts. You've hardly come near me since, well, since last week.'

'Yeah. About that. To be honest I've had a really hard job of keeping my hands off you if you must know, but I was just trying to give you some space and time to make sure you didn't regret anything. Every night I've come round I've thought, *right, tonight I'm going to say something, I'm going to ask you what you're thinking or I'm just going to kiss you and see what your reaction is*, but every night you looked so miserable that I had cold feet. I

150

was scared you'd say something I didn't want to hear. Tell me again, are you absolutely sure you don't regret last weekend?'

She chewed her lip and shook her head slowly. Mack laughed, 'you might want to tell that to your face. My memory might be a bit hazy, but I'm pretty sure, when you were happy about something you didn't chew your lip and frown.' He pulled her closer and kissed her. 'Look, can I give you some advice. Try not to give yourself a hard time over this. Just go with your instincts and follow your heart rather than your head. You were always good at just doing what felt right and not worrying too much about the consequences. I know there's a lot more at stake if you decide that it's all been a big mistake, but you need to give yourself a chance. The worst thing would be if you didn't even give it a chance just because you felt you should be in more doubt or should be wary of the whole thing. I know I have a vested interest in you following your heart rather than your head, but I need to give this my best shot here or I risk losing you.'

'And what if you have second thoughts?'

'I won't! No way. I messed up once and know how it felt to have been so completely stupid and to lose everything. There's no way I'll mess up again.'

She stared into his eyes, looking for something that told her he was telling the absolute truth, but she knew that was impossible. She knew she'd just have to take the greatest leap of faith she could imagine.'

She desperately wanted to throw herself at him, but she needed him to make the first move this time. As if reading her thoughts he bent down to kiss her, slowly unbuttoning her shirt.

**

They lay in silence. Mack could feel a tension and awkwardness between them. 'What's up?' he asked, stroking her shoulder gently.

She sighed. She wanted to say *nothing, I'm fine,* but she knew Mack wouldn't accept that. There was never any point hiding anything from him. He knew her too well.

'Oh, you know, same old, same old. I don't know why I keep coming back to this. I'm annoyed with *myself* that these thoughts keep running through my head, so God knows, you must be getting sick of it too. I'm still finding it difficult to let go of the past. It's like I bottled all this pain up in a jar inside me and screwed the lid on tight. So tight, there's no chance of it escaping and now it sits like a lump of granite, here in my core,' she said, pointing at her ribs, 'and somewhere underneath there's a layer of happiness which has absolutely no chance of escaping, because it's buried so deep underneath the pain. It's difficult to explain, but it's almost like I'm scared to let go of the pain. It's all I know. I keep telling myself, *just get over it! Let it go and let yourself be happy,* but I don't know, maybe I don't want to feel happy again, either that or I'm afraid to feel happy,' she said, more to herself, than to Mack. 'The pain of that happiness coming crashing down is too hard to bear, so I'd rather never feel it again. Does that make sense or are you mentally backing away from the emotional wreckage that is my life?

He pulled her close into to him. 'Does it feel like I'm backing away? And yes I do get it. No happiness, no chance of getting hurt again, right?'

'Yeah, I guess, something like that, that's what my therapist said anyway' she sighed.

'Your therapist!'

152

'Yeah, my therapist! Problem?'

'No, it's just... you didn't mention it. I would never have thought you were the type to go to a therapist.'

'And I would never have said you were the type to have an affair.'

'Point taken. Sorry,' he said looking sheepish, 'it's not a problem...'

'Glad to hear it. Look it's no big deal. It was in America. Everyone had a therapist. In fact, I was considered weird because I didn't have one. Anyway, I only went to a few sessions. I didn't learn anything new.'

'Look,' he said, propping himself up on his elbow, 'if there's any emotional wreckage lying around, it's my fault and up to me to try and piece it back together, starting here,' he said tracing his fingers over her ribs. He bent down and kissed her gently on her abdomen. 'I'm not getting fed up with us coming back to this conversation. I think you need to keep talking about it to get it out of your system, and it's still early days. Don't be so hard on yourself.'

She gave a weak smile and nodded.

'In fact, Ms. Jones, if you'll bear with me, I have some rather unorthodox and untested methods of my own, which might just help release some of that inner happiness you mentioned.'

He kissed her again on the abdomen. 'Tell me, Ms. Jones, do you feel this pain anywhere else?'

'Here,' she said, pointing at her stomach.

He moved his head down and kissed her stomach gently. 'Anywhere else?'

'Here.' She pointed to the top of her thighs.

'Mmm, I see where you're going with this. Hold on tight, as I have a feeling I might be about to release more than just a layer of happiness where I'm headed.

She let out a giggle.

'You see, it's starting to work already'

'Shut up Mack,' she said, pushing his head down.

Afterwards, as she lay with her head on his chest, she asked him the question which continued to niggle at her. 'How can I be absolutely certain you won't end up doing it again? You did it once, without good reason, so how do you even know you won't do it again?'

'I just know. I get that's really difficult for you to accept because you only have my word for it and my word has meant Jack Shit so far, but it's different now.'

'How?'

'Well, there's no doubt in my mind I want to be with you, not that I really had doubts before, but I now have the benefit of experience. I know how it felt to lose you and I never want to feel like that again, but also, and I'm not sure if this is really the right thing to say, but Lily puts a whole different slant on things. I couldn't bear to lose her either and believe me, I know if I fuck up again, you'll be out of here, taking Lily and my world with you. This might sound stupid but Lily feels like a physical part of me. I can feel her here,' he said, pointing to his chest, 'every minute of every day. Losing her would be like someone ripping my heart out. I'd die, literally. So, you see, you have an extra hold over me, not that you need it, because I have no intention of ever doing anything so stupid ever again. I'd never risk doing anything to hurt her or you. Can you see that?'

She nodded. She knew she'd have to put her trust in him and forget the past if she was to have any shot at happiness in the future.

***

Chapter 11

They stood outside the door. She was about to knock but Lily pushed through them and ran up the hall ahead of them. 'Granny, Grandad,' she yelled.

Mack hesitated.

'Mack?' she asked with a look of concern, 'you look like you've seen a ghost'

'God I feel sick.'

'Good! Now you know how I feel,' she said, placing a hand protectively over her stomach.

He took her other hand and smiled. 'Come on, we can do this. I can't imagine they're going to be over the moon, but they can't think any worse of me and I'm fully armed with a fine bottle of Chablis to mellow them if all else fails.'

She looked at the bottle. 'Nice touch. You remembered they love that wine. Shame I can't have any. Right here goes,' she said, gripping his hand to steady her nerves.

Her mother appeared in the hallway, smiling, although her faced hardened slightly when she saw Mack. 'Jen, what are you doing hovering at the door? Come in out of the cold. Lily says you have some exciting news.'